SHAZMAAN-E-SHAB

A rare moon of night

NISHA SAARSAR

pencil

ISBN 978-93-5610-578-2
© NISHA SAARSAR 2022
Published in India 2022 by Pencil

A brand of

One Point Six Technologies Pvt. Ltd.
123, Building J2, Shram Seva Premises,
Wadala Truck Terminal, Wadala (E)
Mumbai 400037, Maharashtra, INDIA
E connect@thepencilapp.com
W www.thepencilapp.com

Author biography

About the Author

Shazmaan-e-shab is the first novel written by Nisha Saarsar. She was born on 19 November 1996 in Chandigarh. She did her graduation and Post-graduation from MCM DAV college for women, Chandigarh, Panjab University. She has a special interest in literature. She has translation skills. Since she has a passion for learning new languages. She is familiar with Urdu, and Persian(dialects).

During her college days, She wrote several articles for the yearbook of college. She also loves to write poetry.

CONTENTS

Chapter 1.

"Fateh Mubarak (Happy Victory) Dadash (Brother)....!
I still can't understand you! Why do you never keep your right on what you get? There is something in your mind that you hide from me."
Why do you stay so silent? What is the reason for this...Dadash (brother)?
"Belief and time Riza!" Shazmaan said.
'What do you mean? I don't understand ... Prince'
'Riza you were very young when our own Vâledeyn (parents) suddenly went missing. You were just a few months old and I was 7 years old …. Ammu Baba took you in his lap and brought us with him to Zahedan. I asked him every time about Maman and Baba but he always remains silent. We both grew up in an upbringing of Ammu Baba, but Riza I always feel the absence of our parents. All this wealth and fame is vain without them and now…you are my only wealth..! I have spent time with Maman and saw her but you haven't seen her properly, "I can't believe in God….Riza ...!" Shazmaan said inconsolably.
Riza's eyes moistened.
"What do you think Riza? Life is easy? …No not at all. Ammu Baba who never got married! Do you know why? …For both of us. He lived his life only for us and still living it. Baba is not here, Maman is not here, but at this

time he is more than our parents to us. If he wasn't with us, perhaps we would have been fighting in the streets of Zahedan to live every day, he ceded his everything to us. I will never forget his favors. But so far I couldn't do anything for him so that he and his soul can get some peace."

"I think your victory should celebrate now …." Riza smiled and said to Shazmaan.

'Our victory Riza …' Shazmaan said while hugging Riza.

Shazmaan adores Riza to his everything. Riza is equally valuable to him as a child is meant to be for their parents. Shazmaan has settled the sultanate, not for himself but for Riza. Shazmaan is everything to Riza. The people of the Sultanate exemplify their love. Even for a moment, both of them could not be separated from each other. Seeing their love, Ammu Baba was also happy and often advised Shazmaan to settle in his new world.

Shazmaan was a lively prince. He was not addicted to alcohol and debauchery like other princes. From Qasr-e-kand to Bazman his Sultanate was extended and Zahedan Sultanate was conquered by Shazmaan's father where certain decisions were taken and in Qasr-e-kand Shazmaan was living with Riza, Ammu Baba. He was a kind-hearted person and also a pure heart. Everything was given by the mercy of God. But still, there was a restlessness in his heart that he probably didn't even know. Because of his ability, Shazmaan got immense love and fame but still, there was some emptiness, and to get rid of this emptiness, he used to colloquy often with his Ammu Baba.

'Salam Ammu Baba! Haal-e-Shoma Chetor ast? (How are you, Baba)?'

"Khoobam! (I am fine) Shukra Khuda va Mubarak ….

(Thank God... and congratulations)

"Thank you very much! Your blessings are always with us."

'Of course my child ….'

'You have won ... yet there is no happiness on your face ... What is the reason why you are so silent and joyless ..?

"You know that I can't forget that night, never ….And to keep our sultanate safe, we have to fight with enemies which always results in victory. But now I am tired of all this, Baba! I find this life strange, I feel some emptiness. I am living life but not just by my own will....! There is no life even without Vâledeyn,

Baba … .No, everything seems strange, and the world seems stranger to me….!"

"This consideration makes you different from other princes. You are different, Shazmaan…! And if you are the only one, who is disappointed, then what about your people and Riza, whom you love the most in the world? … Only you are their courage and strength Also! Life is not so long, Shazmaan! You have a lot to see now; don't know when God will show his mercy on you? You need a good partner. Who will teach you a new way of living life and now I am getting too old. Don't know how many years will I live ..!"

"Don't say that may God keep you safe and sound. Who is ours except you? Your instructions are very important for us Baba and your support too! But marriage … not at all … I can fight with enemies but cannot think of life like marriage"

"But it is important…! Shazmaan How long you will live alone like this and now Riza has also become marriageable. Now don't worry about anything, God is merciful....has given everything and made both of you brothers capable. Nothing more is needed than this, just ask God for the best companion for you. Ardashir is also living his life very comfortably, you should learn from him. He doesn't need to do anything, God also blessed him with good children and because of many marriages his sultanate is everywhere."

"Baba .... How much the life of Sultan Ardashir's life has become limited with his children...He is so busy that if he does not care for you then how he will care about me ....

I have heard that even his elder prince is continuing to build his new sultanate?"

"There is a difference of only one year between yours and his son's age and God has given him two sons even further?"

"Baba, you don't even get married and you instruct us to get married, may I know what was the reason?"

Baba was caressing the white birds

"Spiritual love and Ibadati Eshq, only to God, to nature and Kader (creator)..."

"Do you believe in God ...?"

"Of course ..! And you should too ...."

"Hhhh .... Merciless God ...." said Shazmaan with a different smile.

Shazmaan's Ammu Baba always praised God and used to mention God in every matter. But Shazmaan does not like it all. And there is only one name. Those who take it only for peace of mind and Shazmaan did not have peace of mind, so it was not that easy for Shazmaan never try to mention God's name.

All the time the mind was surrounded by questions! Wish the answer to these could be easily found if Shazmaan tried to ask this question to someone.

Chapter 2.

Green–filled, sitting on a sheet of colored flowers, on small hills a beautiful and full of simplicity, a woman was admiring nature, was lost perhaps her hearts minds whirlwind of praising Kader (who made nature).

"Don't know how he will be who has gifted us such a beautiful world. Heard...! That the one who lives in your protection will never be alone. He is neither afraid of losing nor gaining anything. Still, God, I feel myself alone. Alas! Wish I have Maman also, who loves me like Farzin's Maman, who also hides me in her paradise-like lap, by taking away my all sorrow... I should also have Baba everywhere for my protection, but heard that orphans have only God and my God is an infidel who silently humiliates me every day by Khalejan... merciless God. . "

"Princess Shab Are you here or lost somewhere ... This is evening time and your absence in a palace will stir up a new scene again. Don't know, what you see here?" Sahar said.

Sahar was the personal maid of Princess Shab, but the relationship between the two was more than sisters. There was only one person whom Shab could call her own; otherwise, her own family made her a stranger. Everyone wanted that Shab should get married so that there would be no disturbance among the people that this Sultanate has been taken away from Shab which is the inheritance of her father. Even Shab was not interested in all this; she just wanted to live a comfortable life where someone considers her more than herself.

"You know that Sultan Naveed is looking for a new companion for you. I am very happy for you and pray to God that you get the best partner in the world and you should not have to suffer the troubles you have to bear here.

Heard ... he is the Prince of Zahedan! For whom the princesses of the whole country are ready for Ezdevaaj (marriage)! As God's will, you will be his first wife! Sahar expressed his happiness.

"The first wife ....? What do you mean Sahar? I mean you know very well that I do not like these words at all, Is woman a thing that came not a choice then married another and If not the second then the third and this cycle continues. Does one man become the greatest sultan by marrying many women? Don't know what kind of mentality is this? "

"   Bebakhshid (Pardon me), princess ..." Sahar gets stunned.

"Now tell me, do I look like a princess, look at my dress and see me, do I deserve any prince? Shab asked Sahar laughing and Sahar again start to feel happy.

"It's just that I know that what you are .... And other princesses cannot be like you... Our Maman has said that you speak just like your Vâledeyn. Only you are the promising as every princess should be. You have the skill to handle the Sultanate. "Sahar said proudly.

"If required, then I will handle the Sultanate too, Sahar! But promise me that you will be always with me.

"Promised princess ..."

Just then a serviceman comes toward the princess and tells her to be present in the palace as soon as possible.

"Salaam Shahzadi, Sultan Naveed wants to meet you immediately!"

"Alright, I'll be there!"

Sultan Naveed was waiting for Shab in a meeting room near the garden of the palace.

"Salaam Dadash, is everything okay?"

"All is good, how are you?"

"I always feel safe in your kingship and you know this better than me," said Shab with a smile.

"May God bless you with all happiness?"

"Mamnoon (Thank you)"

"I have something to tell you"

"Say Dadash"

"Shab, now I have to take an important decision in your life!"

Many questions were visible in Shab's eyes. She didn't understand anything. The important decision in life, don't know what new trouble is going to come now. Shab believed this.

"Dadash dear, have I done anything wrong?" Shab said nervously.

"No Shab, but first promise me that you will obey our every word and my order"

"But till date, I have not disobeyed any of your orders!"

"I want you're Ezdevaaj (marriage) to be completed with the prince of Zahedan, Shazmaan!"

"But Dadash, I am not ready for all this yet"

"Shab you are our responsibility!"

"No, I am so capable that I don't want to be anyone's responsibility."

"Shab, I have taken the decision and then all the princesses accept this life. I know that your dreams are different but believe me, there can be no better Queen for Shazmaan than you. There is more ability in you than what is in Shazmaan. I only know that there is no other person like you in Nikshahar! I won't say anything more than that. I have sent a message to Zahedan and have also kept a feast for both the princes. Hope you will not be unhappy with our decision. The rest of the decision is not going to change because it is heard that Prince Shazmaan is looking for a partner with similar qualities as he has. " Naveed said

"But Dadash Jaan, I do not have any merits," Shab said while acting.

"Shab I feel that you know yourself better than me. You hold a lot of information, maybe so much that no one else has and one day this information will make your every problem easy."

Naveed was the Sultan of Nikshahar and half-brother of Farzin. But Shab who was the daughter of the great Sultan, Naveed wanted to rule all her sultanate and her rights, only on his own, so he wanted a sending off of Shab as soon as possible so that no one would have any doubts and also gets successful in this trick. But still, he used to respect Shab somewhere but the holdings of Shab were better than Shab, Shab knew it because for Shab all this was just a heap of mud, nothing more. The true wealth of the world is only her parents - in front of whom this whole world is nothing.

But don't know how much happiness and sadness are written in God's articles, Only God knows and no one else, just as we have to fight such conditions of life. That's just the consideration of Shab.

Chapter 3.

Near the lattice panjere (window), two white birds were chatting in the light of the setting sun. A Fragrance was in the air and there was a light reddish color in the sky. White clouds were now pink. Birds are flying independently in the sky, don't know what they got? Sometimes they used to sit on the highest peak of the white buildings and sometimes they go out to measure the sky. It is time for the arrival of the moon, which makes this palace even more beautiful with its light. Many fragrant flowers are planted in the garden of the palace and along with it, there was a gathering of fireflies. How beautiful a view is this! Shazmaan alone was watching this scene. Then Riza came to the garden looking for him.

"Asr be kheyr ! Prince Shazmaan" said Riza.

"Oh! ….Riza is everything alright and what is this in your hand? Shazmaan asked.

"This is the Invitation from Sultan Naveed of Nikshahar for the feast and …"

"And ...?" Shazmaan said.

"And Ezdevaaj.

"Whose Ezdevaaj (marriage)"? Shazmaan asked in amazement.

"Mine and ..."

"Riza, tell me exactly what the matter is and why there is the discussion about Ezdevaaj?" Shazmaan asked Riza

Riza had met Farzin earlier. Since then he has started loving Farzin and he had told this thing to his Ammu Baba that he would not choose anyone other than Farzin as his companion, on the other hand, Farzin had also accepted Riza as her everything. But Ammu Baba wanted that Shazmaan should get married first before Farzin and Riza. But for that first Shazmaan's choice was very important and Ammu Baba knew very well about Sultan Naveed's message, so he did not consider it appropriate to think too far. Ammu Baba came to know about Shab and liked the discussion of her simplicity and he said " Yes" to Sultan Naveed's Invitation, and didn't delay in sending the answer. But what will Shazmaan say on this, will he agree for Ezdevaaj?

"Dadash, I love the princess of Nikshahar Farzin ..." Riza stopped saying this.

"Very good! so you want to marry her," said Shazmaan with a smile.

"Dadash... but Ammu Baba wants you to get married first and then we will!" Riza said

"Riza you know that ..." Then Riza interrupts him.

"Dadash dear, what is wrong in this, it is the decree of God to live your life and then this is the principle of life."

"Riza... Ezdevaaj is a big decision in life itself and a responsibility which I ..." Then Ammu Baba comes there and says to Shazmaan.

"Life is unique, sometimes clouds of sorrow rain and sometimes the light of happiness spreads and you will never get a better chance than this one. Shahzadi Shab is a deserving and promising princess and she will prove to be a good Mallika if both of you get to know and understand each other better. I tried to know about Princess Shab and found that nothing can be better than her. She has many qualities like every single Mallika should have. But if your decision remains the same then maybe this will be a burden on my soul after death. It will always be that I could not teach Shazmaan the real meaning of life in the right way. If you have someone else in your mind, another princess or any girl in the sultanate, then tell us! But keep in mind that a sultan cannot become a sultan without Ezdevaaj nor can he handle his sultanate! I cannot explain to you more than this, only a few days are left of my life and your wish is ahead!" by Saying this Ammu Baba left from there.

"I will wait for your decision, Dadash Jaan," said Riza and left.

As if Ammu Baba had hit home on Shazmaan's heart and mind or may have awakened his conscience that now gets up.

After a moment of silence, a question arose again in his mind how did Riza fall in love? He never mentioned and decided to get married so soon?

"It is also good that Riza has chosen a companion for himself whom he knows very well but I do not even know her ….. Why the world has created such customs?

And on the other hand, Ammu Baba…If I don't fulfill his wish, maybe my soul hates me too that I have disobeyed Ammu Baba. If Ammu Baba wants this Ezdevaaj then I'm ready and that's what Riza wants too. Ammu Baba has done a lot for us and for the first time he asked me for something but don't know ... why Ezdevaaj is needed to be a Sultan? The sultanate can be maintained even without Ezdevaaj and our people are happy too. They don't have any problem. Damn it, the confusion of our mind never ends..... Don't know why this heart reminds me of that day?

Chapter 4.

Ardashir who was the Shazmaan's Ammejade (Shazmaan's uncle's son), ruled in Mashhad, had spread his sultanate far with his five wives and their three Dokhtar (daughters), seven Pesar (son or prince) were living their life happily together.

Ardashir's fifth wife was from the Arab country, very beautiful, but seeing her eyes, it seemed that she was very clever and a trickster. Ardashir had the youngest son and he was the little innocent prince of Mashhad, very dear to sultan Ardashir. All princes of the Sultan were ruling different parts of Persia - but Ardashir's life was very good with the little prince, for living the rest of his life, Ardashir didn't need anything.

Because of his Arabian wife, he established his rule very well on many sultanates, and by getting the rest of his son's marriage to the princesses of the Arab country, he was living life easily. He was proud of his wife Sultana. But in the heart of Sultana, there was something else.

Zahedan was a beautiful sultanate and for many years Sultana had an eye there. Hearing the praises of the well-formed prince of this beautiful city, she had to grab the sultanate too.

For many years, Persia was doing merchandise their wares in Arabic countries and many things also came from Hind through trade... This could have happened only by the sea and through horses from India. Many types of things were sent or ordered to each other's countries. Because of the increasing speed of trade, ships were made which were capable of carrying heavyweight in the sea. These ships could easily move from one end to the other. It was easy to cover the distance of miles. This was the best way to do business. Grapes were the most traded in Arab countries, where their demand is still the same as it was before.

And all are drawn to this beautiful city, Sultana wished that if she was Shazmaan's companion then she wouldn't take her time to achieve all this, but she was already someone else's. Who is much older than her? Neither she was in love with Ardashir, nor her child, she just loved fame and wealth. Somewhere she used to like Shazmaan too, but now probably because of his fame. She could easily achieve anything by plotting, it had become her profession. No one can catch her red-handed because of her clever mind. Sultana was closer to Ardashir than the rest of Ardashir's wives. Through her gimmicks, she slowly trapped Ardashir in her nets and began to settle down the people of her country. Other sultans like Ardashir also believed that Arabs are settled here only and only for business, nothing more than this.

As soon as Sultana talks to Ardashir about Shazmaan, "Shazmaan's name has become famous from Zahedan to Mashhad and even then why not the prince is so capable. Heard! That Shazmaan is ready for Ezdevaaj, why not we should complete my sister Asma's Ezdevaaj with Shazmaan."

Ardashir said, "But I had heard that Shazmaan never wanted to get married, so how did all this happen suddenly."

"Sultan-e-Ali now whatsoever is happening is good. Isn't it?" sultana said.

"But his marriage has been fixed with someone else, Sultana!" Ardashir said

"Means …. What are you saying? Asking this, Sultana stopped and started thinking about how to stop this marriage and if she went to Zahedan, it would take her about 7 days to reach there and there is no time to send a message. If Asma was Shazmaan's first wife, then how good it would have been because the first wife would have a status higher than the rest of the wives or to say that the first wife is equal to a sultan. But I'll find a way for this too. Sultana sends a message to her sister to come to Zahedan and Asma also agrees to come to Zahedan as soon as she received the message.

Sultana could not tolerate whatever she had her eye on; she could easily let it go. Sultana requests Ardashir that she wants to go to Zahedan but Sultana didn't tell Ardashir anything about Asma.

She says to Ardashir, "By the way, everyone will be invited to Shazmaan's Ezdevaaj and we will be specially invited for the Dawat, so why not leave from here for Zahedan in advance."

"It is not right for me to leave such a huge sultanate and people, Sultana. If you want to go there then you are allowed but I want you to take Hassan with you, he will also roam in Zahedan, then he will also like it very much, but only for a few days. Dawat (feast of a wedding) may take longer but you cannot reach Zahedan before that.

"Ardashir said

"That's why I want to go early so that I can be there by the time of the feast. ' said Sultana

"Baleh (yes) you are allowed but as you know, Hassan is very dear to me, so it is your responsibility to take good care of him. You know I can't live long without him. "Ardashir said

Sultana was happy because she would go there with Asma and will start her new game, which is her nature.

Chapter 5.

The light of Aftab (sun) was spreading goldenness on the face of Prince Shazmaan. There is something special in this Morning. This has never happened before. Again those two white words were sitting at the window. As if they were saying with love to Shazmaan 'get up now.' This air... Yes, this air is the same aromatic as that day. Shazmaan was feeling everything different - Then Riza came into his room.

"Sobh be kheyr (good morning) Dadash!"

"Ah! Riza! ... So early morning?"

"Dadash we have to go Nikshahar today .... And Sir is still resting, come on get up now."

"Riza ... Riza listen to me... First, tell me how you came to know Farzin and you didn't tell me that you liked her too! Where did you meet her?"

"Dadash ... Do You remembers, one or two months before there was a competition of... Asvswari (horse riding)! That's where Farzin met me and since then we like each other. I didn't tell you because it was my obstinacy that you should find a partner for yourself before me. I used to chat with Farzin through letters and Farzin told me that Sultan Naveed wants to meet us at a special feast. I informed Ammu Baba and he also first discussed your Ezdevaaj with Sultan Naveed and Sultan Naveed informed me about Shahzadi Shab. As you know, for Ammu Baba, nothing can be better than it, and then he asked to go ahead with this matter so that you too can meet the princess. But I'll marry Farzin when you will find someone special for you, whether she is Princess Shab or someone else."

"Riza why are you dragging me with your happiness ...... you know that I can hardly like anyone, and then it is a distant matter of Ezdevaaj," Shazmaan said

"Dadash Jaan, I know that you have never been interested in anything except war, people, and country, but life is also a war that has to be lived or fought with only one companion and this life is like a kayak that can be Difficult to drive alone."

"You have grown up and started talking like Ammu Baba ... khoob (very well)"

"So let's get ready as soon as possible ... we'll be late," Riza said.

"I am always ready for you ... Riza. Only for you" Shazmaan thought in his mind.

"What are you thinking Dadash? ... You always think about my happiness but today I'm praying for the happiness of your life, to get married and I hope that you will never refuse me. "Riza said

"Riza, I will marry only that princess who has the skill, manner, and who is well-versed in the laws and regulations of the Sultanate and the people! Are your princesses like this?" Shazmaan said while acting smartly.

"Only God can give you such a princess and no one else! As far as Farzin is seen, Shahzadi Shab is very different and simple. Your sultanate will not be lost by seeing once, and for God's sake come with us. "Riza said while laughing and left with Shazmaan and Ammu Baba for Nikshahar.

The border of Nikshahar was crossed soon and an aroma of the pleasant rose gardens was coming from far away. A huge business of rose perfume used to start from here. Roses were the hallmark. Water wells were easily found in Nikshahar, from where roses and many types of fruits were cultivated. With time, Nikshahar also started smelling like flowers. There was greenery everywhere where felt a sense of relief- All the worries of the world were lost after coming to the Nikshahar.

"Hairat Avar (wonderful)! When the city is so beautiful then… How beautiful will the people here and the princesses be too? Did I say right, Dadash?" Riza asked Shazmaan

"But only you know everything about here, very well, and also about the princess Farzin. Whether Farzin is beautiful or not, how can I tell you Riza ..?"

"I was talking about Princess Shab but you didn't understand my gesture …" said Riza.

"You are bothering me, Riza ..."

"Bebakhshid Shahzade" Riza started laughing loudly while saying.

"Will you both keep quiet for a moment, soldiers of this city are standing in front of us to welcome us, just behave gently," said Ammu Baba.

And then in a loud voice, all soldiers said, "Khoshamdid Shahzade Shazmaan wa Shahzade Riza may your dignity be high, thank you very much." Saying all the soldiers and servants of the palace and made a way for them to enter the palace, the path, decorated with rose flowers. That path was going straight to the big gate of the palace. The view of that palace was mesmerizing, the white-colored palace on which the golden carving is done." There was a striped carving. The palace's windows were also carved, it was very beautiful. There is a Place on the walls of the castle for birds. There were beautiful gardens around the palace with a variety of fruits and flowers. "I have never seen such beauty before", said Shazmaan.

"This place is really beautiful ..." said Riza.

Only then Sultan Naveed appears from the front.

"Khoshamdi, khoshamdi, thank you so much from the bottom of my heart for accepting my message." Sultan Naveed said

"Salaam Sultan Naveed" said Shazmaan and Riza

" Jiba ...." said Sultan Naveed while looking at Shazmaan. Ammu Baba hugged Sultan Naveed. Ammu Baba advised Sultan Naveed to talk privately and Sultan Naveed went to a room for special guests with Ammu Baba. He said to the servants, "Both the princes should be taken for a walk of the palace and there shouldn't be any kind of shortage in their service."

After sitting silently for a while, Sultan Naveed said to Ammu Baba, "So what is your decision ..?"

"Hmm .... From Riza's side, I have to say "yes" but right now it is difficult to decide for Shazmaan. I believe that Shazmaan does not want to disobey me, that's why he's with us. But Sultan Naveed! it is a little difficult for me to decide in the case of Ezdevaaj. But I hope Shab has no issues with Ezdevaaj. "Ammu Baba said

"Not at all ... Shab has no issue ... Though she is very happy ... If you have permission, I would like to give the order to present both the princes in front of the princesses ... as it is a tradition. Only the princes are shown in front of princesses. "Sultan Naveed said.

"Of course, it is allowed… by now both the princes must have visited the palace." Ammu Baba said.

The princesses were called and then the princes after them. All this was happening very quickly as if someone wanted that it should not be too

Late! Don't know where life will turn next. Time is short and life is too short, be successful in your goal as soon as possible, don't miss anything!

Shazmaan said yes or no, Shab did not know because for a moment Shab did not even look at Shazmaan lifting her eyelids. You will know now or later, but Shazmaan caught a glimpse of Shab and then Ammu Baba as if Ammu Baba has said a lot. Shazmaan said "Yes" for Ezdevaaj as Ammu Baba lowered his eyelids and raised him again. A little happiness in the eyes of Ammu Baba and is proud on his face that Shazmaan had seen. He wanted to hug Shazmaan. Shazmaan in their eyes now got a good heart prince; understood the meaning of life, Ammu Baba and Shazmaan were just gesturing with sight, at that time Sultan Naveed said...

"I am very happy that Prince Shazmaan and Riza will be our son-in-law...Damad-e-Nikshahar. I want that after 2 days we should schedule the time for Ezdevaaj."

"A ..... a.. .... isn't it too early Sultan ... ? "Shazmaan said.

"Of course, it will be the right time ..." said Ammu Baba.

"But ..." said Shazmaan

"I know that no one will be bothered by this," Baba said

"Sultan Naveed allow us .... Evening time is going to over," Baba said to Sultan Naveed and left from there.

"Sultan Naveed ... I am very happy with your decision ... I like Farzin's choice but Shab for Shazmaan? ... It took me a little strange. I believe that someone else can be better for him but not Shab ..." said Farzin's Maman.

"Maman, why do you always care about only and only for Farzin, you already know that Shab has no one except us, and now Shab has also become worldly-wiser. She has too right to have some happiness. Till today you couldn't give her love, and today is the right time to take an important decision in her life ... maybe this is not acceptable for you... You know very well that Shab is much better than Farzin and I think for Shab, no one can be better than Shazmaan. Shazmaan is not like those princes who do too many marriages to become famous or to expand the Sultanate's borders. He respects humanity and our country respects emotions instead of jealousy. No one is like Shazmaan and Riza. Shazmaan didn't rebel ever; he has just made his kingdom with love, Humans like him are rarely seen, otherwise, only the deviant sultan or prince can be seen on our land. "Naveed said to Farzin's Maman said "Now that this is your decision, I should not ask more questions. ' said Farzin's mother.

"Remember one thing, Maman, our Valedayan, who was your husband and our late Maman, has always served the late Sultan of Nikshahar, and knowing that the first right on this Sultanate was of Shab, she was living a simple life, not as a princess. If she wants, she can ask for all this from me only tomorrow, but no! She didn't. And don't get so excited for God's sake that later you become a victim of your misery. Khuda Hafiz!" Saying this, Sultan Naveed left from there.

"Don't know why he always praises Shab? Well may only God knows .... ,

Farzin's mother was the second wife of Sultan Naveed's father. She wanted Sultan Naveed to think only for Farzin and not pay attention to Shab, which she used to do with Shab, but Shab accepted it as a part of her life. And she did not complain about life and never with Sultan Naveed. There was no one to understand Shab except Sultan Naveed and a servant Sahar and no one else. Maybe she sacrificed her right for the sake of Sultan Naveed because this is a worldly show, the real Wealth was snatched from her in childhood, and now this long breath of life was going on unnecessarily, perhaps God has yet to show a lot and what should be the purpose of life? Why should it live? This is also left.

"This is called life
Which we live on our terms
But it teaches its
way of living. "

Chapter 6.

"Shahzadi Shab, many beautiful gifts come to the palace today and you will be very happy to know from where these gifts were sent!" Sahar said very happily.

"Aha! Gifts and for me, this has never happened before ….!" Shab said while making fun of Sahar.

" Hmmm you know that Shazmaan sent these gifts for you and I had already got all these in your room, it has a special dress to wear at the time of marriage and many more nuts and fruits and also jewelry and … . Yes, this jewelry - is made of silver and gold as you will be the first wife of Shazmaan, he sent this Sarband, studded with pearls ...... oh I'm sorry princess that I used these words again, I shouldn't say this and even you didn't stop me today …. Shahzadi Shab! Are you listening … Shahzadi Shab!" Sahar spoke into the ear of the lost Shab and said

"Oh, please speak slowly …." Shab said

"Are you thinking of something?"

"Baleh (yes)! I was thinking that everything is happening very quickly, do not know what will be the consequence."

"Consequence! What do you mean? I don't understand, and what is the relation of consequence with Ezdevaaj (marriage)?"

"How much I know Shazmaan, I mean I didn't even see him, and the way Farzin and Riza know each other very well, not like that! Then saying yes raises many questions in my mind, maybe later he wouldn't give me any kind of attention! Have you noticed I wasn't in royal dress and he is going to be the sultan of such a big sultanate! What did he see in me? I don't deserve him…Sahar! I feel nervous by thinking it over and over again."Shab expressed.

"If I see prince Shazmaan, I don't think so …. well I want to give you a piece of advice… don't think too much and I am always with you … here and in Qasr - e - Kand too, you will not face any kind of problem. God is with you for your protection!"

"Mamnoon(Thank You) Sahar!

"I don't have time, be ready, I will take care of your important stuff … Prince Shazmaan and Riza will be coming soon! And I'm calling maiden to adore our beloved Arus (the bride) as soon as possible."

According to the Persian rituals, everything was arranged which is necessary for an Agd (wedding). The Palace was looking so beautiful, decorated with flowers. It wasn't less than a festival. After all, it was the marriage of the famous prince Shazmaan. Sultans from different cities were invited. The Separate stages were made for Riza and Farzin; just there were waiting for the princes.

" Wow! Prince Shazmaan is so graceful. He has sky blue eyes. God made him dashing, with a beautiful mind." Sahar expressed

While coming to the palace, Shazmaan again felt the same fragrance that often he felt and the same beautiful white birds were giddy in the sky.

"Don't know why all this happening to me but ... it is a different feeling! The heart wants me to get lost in this fragrance and forget all the worries of the world." Shazmaan said while talking to himself.

"Dadash first is your turn …." Riza said
"My turn ...?" Shazmaan said ignorantly like he doesn't know anything.
"It is the custom to see your partner in the mirror …. Before that … you cannot see the face of your partner ….,
" Riza…!" Shazmaan said shyly.
And thus Shazmaan and Riza got married with all the rituals. Ammu Baba, Sultan Naveed, and all were happy. Farzin and Shab were looking very beautiful. Shab's face was shining in the golden dress, just like gold.
For a while, Farzin's Maman (Mother) came to her room with Farzin.
Farzin my dear girl you look so beautiful! I'm here with you because I want to tell you something important. Soon there will be your send-off and now Shab is the wife of Shazmaan. Everyone will give importance to Shab. But I want you shouldn't give her any kind of attention. If she tries to order you then don't listen to her or you can disobey her. Despite this, if she rules, then leave no stone unturned to humiliate her, it will separate the Shazmaan and Shab. Try these tricks which I have taught you."
"From the first day, I did not want that Shab also goes to the same place where I am going, again the same heart-wrenching things will happen, Shab, Shab and just Shab …! Don't know why Sultan Naveed took such a decision, if he wants, he could fix Shab's Ezdevaaj elsewhere, but why here, now I have to see her face every day. I don't

know what's wrong with him?"
Farzin said angrily.

"Don't worry, you will find a way for this too. After a few days, I will try to convince Riza that he should maintain his sultanate in Qasr-e-kand itself and Shazmaan should be in Zahedan, and then you will never have to see Shab. "Farzin's Maman said.

"I want also the same; Maman, but Riza will never leave Shazmaan. Shazmaan is very dear to Riza and it is impossible to separate them. And then I have no problem with Prince Shazmaan, I have a problem with Shab and I will find a way out for that." Farzin said.

Farzin did not care about those who admired Shab; she was also bored with the name of Shab when Shab was mentioned in everything. Shab had the skills to handle the sultanate but Farzin only loves her beauty. Shab used to ease every difficulty that came on the people in a few moments. The whole people wanted only Shab except for Farzin and Farzin's respect. That's why Farzin started disliking Shab And Shab used to love Farzin as much as whether Farzin was talking to her or not.

Chapter 7.

Seven days have passed since the princess has come to Qasr-e-Kand, not even once she could face Shazmaan. Whenever Shab saw Riza and Farzin, she liked it very much. But Shazmaan did not even talk about Shab's well-being till now.

"Sahar, I feel that Prince Shazmaan does not like me. Look at Riza and Farzin, with each other, how happy they are! I wish Dadash had not married me; I would not have been sitting like this. Today, seven days have passed since Ezdevaaj was completed. I feel that maybe I am a burden on him or our presence hurts him." Shab said inconsolably to Sahar.

"Don't worry about that princess! Shahzade Shazmaan will talk to you and I think you should start first."
"… no not at all, I am afraid of him … I can't talk … and he should talk first, not me…,
"Then you have to just wait and wait!"
"Sahar! For a few days, let's go to the Nikshahar, I want to meet Dadash, before leaving I want that a message should be sent to Dadash, he would be delighted to see…" Shab said.
"But before that, we have to get permission from Prince Shazmaan. Without his permission, this is not possible and

I have heard that the message of the wife of Sultan Ardashir, who is Prince Shazmaan's cousin, has arrived. I think she can reach the palace by today, maybe to congratulate you on your marriage. In such a situation, it is not possible to go to Nikshahar. This is against the customs." Sahar informed Shab.

" But my heart says to go there and just tell me how can anyone live here, Farzin does not talk to me and since the time of Ezdevaaj, she also dislikes my presence and Because of whom I am here, he didn't even ask me that how I am? Only Ammu Baba and Prince Riza's behavior is best for me. I feel as if I am in captivity where there is no fresh climate." Shab expressed her feeling.

"If you say, I can ask for permission from Prince Shazmaan !" Sahar said.
"You can try"
It was dusk and prince Shazmaan, Riza, and Ammu Baba were chatting in the garden.
"I am very glad that you did not disobey me. " Ammu Baba said to Shazmaan
"Your disobedience is equal to self-hurting, Baba," Shazmaan said
"Now it won't be difficult to go to God's abode, " Ammu Baba said
"What are you talking about, Baba? You are dear to us and only you are only our life support, if you say so, we will be broken."
"Dear! First, did you talk to your partner or not?
" A ...... Baba .... that ..... I .... but wanted to talk ....
. "Shazmaan's words were incomplete.

Then Riza and Baba burst out laughing.

"We didn't question anything wrong Dadash ...that you are shying and there is no need to be so flustered !" Riza said.

"I got it … .Shazmaan it is very difficult for you to talk to a Girl... and it becomes even more difficult when someone is a stranger to us. For that, you have to make her your friend first. A special friend causing your pain, and discomfort, can mention her grief and happiness. And the most important is to respect each other... I know that the decision Ezdevaaj is difficult for you, but now you have to perform it! Maybe you can get answers to some of your questions. "Ammu Baba said.

Then a steward presents a message to prince Shazmaan, Along with the news of the arrival of Ardashir's wife Sultana, there are also greetings of marriage.

"What is written in this message …?" Riza and Ammu Baba said.

"Today, Zan - e - Ardashir is coming to the palace," Shazmaan said.

"This is a new problem." Ammu Baba said.

"What! What did you say, Baba?" Riza said.

"Nothing … Riza but I don't like Sultana at all and I don't like her coming." Ammu Baba said thoughtfully.

"But nobody can be stopped from coming. Anyway, she is our guest, the royal guest," said Shazmaan.

"Baleh! You have said it right but still, I would say that you have to be careful everywhere, Shazmaan." Ammu Baba said while looking into the eyes of Shazmaan.

"As you say".

Ammu Baba goes out for a walk in the garden. Riza wanted to ask Shazmaan a lot but he could not dare. Riza knew that Shazmaan doesn't rest in his room since Ezdevaaj and was not even present at mealtime. He used to roam alone here and there in the palace. Seeing Shazmaan silent, Riza could not stop himself and he extruded the question from his mind.

"I'm sorry, Dadash Jaan ...!" Riza said.

"Riza…! For what?" Shazmaan asked.

"To make you sleepless and to take comfort from your life with my obstinacy, to make your smile disappear and not to obey your heart and to sacrifice your happiness just because of my obstinacy...." Riza said.

Shazmaan stares at Riza in astonishment and silently.

"Riza is everything alright? What happened to you? Just a while back you were fine then why are you saying all this?" Shazmaan asked Riza.

"It's enough Dadash ...am I not seeing you, you have stopped spending time with us and you're starting to get away from all of us ... gradually you are changing your way, you are not present in the palace whenever someone asks about you. You are running away from us." Riza said cheerlessly.

"No Riza it is not like that at all. I believe that you should spend your precious time with Farzin ... not with me."

"And where are you spending your precious time? In this palace, someone is thinking only about you by leaving everything, but you are going away from her too, Dadash! Her life is as important as yours and ours ...." Riza exhorted.

"Riza … I probably can't live with her the way you and Farzin living and no one can know anyone in two days, you too have taken a year to know Farzin. That's why you wanted to marry each other!"
"But a day is enough to know someone Dadash … and you already alienated her"

"Riza you already knew that I don't like all this at all but for the happiness of Ammu Baba, I got it right and like you, I am not interested in worldly appearances like love. You know this better than me and if I talk about Princess Shab, then she wouldn't have any kind of problem here. But you and the princess should not expect me to become a good prince or a sultan who thinks only about his wife and children, without the people and the sultanate. Just see Ammu Baba's life, he did not get married too, but I have done all this only for his happiness and this is a very small renunciation for him. I will be always grateful for what they have done for us." Shazmaan explained.

"You are calling your partner a renunciation, Dadash! I'm surprised that you are the same Shazmaan, who never let a bird get scratched, But you are giving someone's life the name of renunciation, you are so mean! It was my fault that I took a long time to understand you. Your thinking... made me surprised. That's why you can't love and respect anyone."

Riza said this and started leaving from there looking back, the princess Shab and Sahar were standing there listening to the conversation. Shab's face was full of tears, there were no words to say anything, and her face was asking only one thing "why".

Riza said to Shab, "I'm sorry, Shahzadi Shab! I didn't know this either."

Shazmaan saw that Shab had heard everything and her eyes were questioning a lot. Then Sahar said to the prince Shazmaan, "Salam to the Sultan of Zahedan! Shahzadi Shab wants permission from you to go to Nikshahar for a few days!"

Shazmaan sees Shab and Shab stands at a distance. Shazmaan says to Sahar, "Allowed but after three days! Inform the princess, that today our special guests will be present in the palace at the time of evening and whatever she has heard, it shouldn't inform Ammu Baba at all. If this happens, both of you will be responsible for his health. Amu Baba and Riza are very dear to me and you should keep them in mind! I don't want them to be in any trouble." Saying this, prince Shazmaan also leaves from there.

 "Sahar I told you that Shazmaan doesn't like me and you have heard it too … It's enough, not anymore Sahar! I want to go back to Nikshahar and will ask Dadash to answer all my questions. why did he do this to me ?" Shab said.

"Princess Shab, be patient. Nothing can be done by being sad like this; it's only a matter of three days."

"But I want to go now! What is here now?" Saying this Shab's eyes turned red.

"Even if we go to the Nikshahar …! Then it would be a defy to the prince Shazmaan."

"That's why I'm away from the issue of marriage, but Naveed Dadash had compelled me … Sahar it is wrong … Can't I live our life on our terms? Why do I need others to make decisions about my life? Is there no importance in my life?"

" Don't be upset princess…trust God, everything will be fine"
" It was better to bear the envy of Farzin and her mother than such imprisonment."
No one has time! Neither time sees Wealth nor poverty. Today is ours, tomorrow someone else's. And this time tells everyone its importance or status, but no one knows the importance of this time and no one appreciates it. And those who are aware of its importance and care about it, so no one cares about them.
This Human considers himself to be very smart, for his own sake, the life of others seems minor to him, but his life is more precious than diamonds and pearls! Human beings are very selfish. But time opens everyone's eyes and shows the truth, no one is more powerful than time except God. Despite knowing this, a person makes all the mistakes and lives a life of lies and lives his life in false pride. This is the reality of life!

Chapter 8.

An old lady was sitting in the little broken house.

"If you remember anything please tell me properly ..... That way I will never be able to find your children. If you are hungry then you eat this apple." Mohsin said to the old lady.

"I only remember Riza… he was very young at that time… but I don't know where he would be at this time. Maybe those sinners killed that little darling." Saying this, the old lady burst into tears.

"Ah… not again Khaleh (aunt)…. Take some peace of mind. Mohsin said.

"Mohsin ... do your work! It is her daily job to cry. Don't know what kind of trouble you have brought… Attend buyers…! Since the time you have brought her, the business is not going well and neither do you like working." Mohsin's owner said.

Mohsin used to work with a Mevdaar (fruit seller). He was only 13 years old. Mohsin had come from far away to earn for living and started living in Dirman. There was a huge demand for nuts in Persia, due to which there were lots of dry-fruits shops in every street. There was a small tenement house, nearby where Mohsin used to live and an elderly woman also lived with Mohsin. Sometimes Mohsin used to call her Maman (Mother) and sometimes Khaleh (aunt). Mohsin would often ask her about herself. So she calls herself the wife of the Great Sultan of Zahedan but Mohsin does not believe her. Mohsin feels that maybe she is a victim of some big accident, that's why she talks like this.

Mohsin was a common man whose job was to sell fruits and vegetables. Sometimes he felt pity for the poor old lady.

"Don't know what kinds of children are those who left their Maman on the way….Once found, I will teach them a good lesson. They have no fear of God...!"
Some circumstances were changing. People's tongues were changing. Where each other was treated with respect, now people did not like to talk to each other ... just hatred for each other and nothing else... The sultans were becoming dissolute.

Two passers-by were talking to each other.
"Know... today again theft has taken place in the Sultanate…."
"Baleh (Yes), it has also been heard that women are being kidnapped and made slaves and sold in other countries also."
"Nine women disappeared overnight, nothing has been found yet."
"So many children have become orphans till now! God bless, we have refused to let our women out. Rest God is the protector…!"

"Maybe the woman's selling..! Our Sultan should make some special laws and regulations to keep the people safe. ,
"All this is a conspiracy by these sultans, they do not take care of their people properly and then these sultans allow

people from outside countries to stay here."
"Now we must protect our children and women by ourselves!"
"

"well said….Young girls should not be left free now….In dark (black) clothes I have seen many such people whose tone does not match us at all, seeing them it seems that they will kill you by their sights …. Big eyes and which are too red and the kohl is so much like the whole mine of kohl is in their eyes. Feel fear whenever see them."
"I feel that an evil time is about to come on our country!"
Saying this, both the passers-by went ahead. Mohsin was listening to them and took the elderly woman back to the tenement house. Fear had also developed in Mohsin's heart.
"Is something is going to happen in our country...! May God bless and keep everyone safe. It has been more than two years, I have not even gone to meet our family yet and then this elderly Maman can't be left alone here. How helpless is the poor person..! maybe someone makes her a slave.!" Mohsin was thinking that only then Mohsin get a voice.
"Mohsin, I'm thirsty….!" the old lady said.

"Oh… have some water….! What happens to you now and then? You are something else in the market and fine here as if nothing happened to you. Is this an incurable disease? Or have you got some shock? Sometimes your tone is like a Mallika and sometimes like an unblessed woman." Mohsin said.
"But I can't remember...what are you talking about?"
"See you forgot again....! You should take a rest, I go to my work."

"Mohsin my child…don't know why I don't remember anything….intentionally I don't want to disturb you."
"Look, you should take a rest…. Thinking too much can affect your brain." saying this Mohsin walks out.

Chapter 9.

"Asalam Walekum! Prince Shazmaan or Baba! We would like to apologize, it took a long time to come but reached before the evening. "Sultana had reached the palace and Asma and Hassan were also present with them.
"Khushamdid (Welcome) Zan-e-Ardashir (wife of Ardashir)! And our dear Hassan." Saying Shazmaan took Hassan in his lap.
"Hope Ardashir is doing well…. He would have been here too!" Ammu Baba said to Sultana.

"Baba everything is alright…we had asked him to accompany us to congratulate Shazmaan but he loves his sultanate very much so I took Asma along!"
"We think you must be tired of traveling… you should take a rest. Shazmaan said to Sultana
"But before that, we want to meet both of your partners…. Shahzade Shazmaan! We will take rest only after seeing them…."

Shazmaan orders the servants to present the princess Shab and Farzin. Ammu Baba and Shazmaan left from there with Hassan. Farzin and Shab arrived there shortly after.
"Wallah! So beautiful…!" Sultana said seeing the princesses and turned to Shab and started seeing her from top to bottom with her own eyes.

"If I guess you are Shab... right?!"

"Baleh Man Shab Hastam (Yes I am Shab)...!" Shab said

"Mashallah, so beautiful....that's why a person like Shazmaan agreed to marry you. What magic did you do?" Shab stands silently.

"Many congratulations to you on starting your new life!" Asma said to Shab.

"Shukran!" Shab said.

"Wallah you know Arabic!" said the Sultan in surprise.

"Not much, just a few words....!" Shab said.

"So meet her, she is my younger sister Asma...."

"Salaam!" Shab said.

"Did you like her?" Sultana asked Shab.

"I don't understand anything...!" Shab said in amazement.

"Hhhh (laughs)......I want Asma to be married to Shazmaan but her status should be of the first wife! By chance, you are Shazmaan's first wife!"

"Are you kidding?" Shab asked Sultana.

Sultana gets silent at once and says looking into Shab's eyes.

"I am not kidding...you have replaced Asma...and I want you to keep your rank lower than her and not first."

"Is Prince Shazmaan also wants so? I mean... did he know this and if he knew, why did he marry me..? Is Shazmaan aware of this matter? Even he didn't want to get married, so then... all this?"

Sultana interrupts Shab.

"You ask a lot of questions... it is my duty to convince Shazmaan... it would be better if you go out of your way! It would be better for all."

Saying this, Sultana and Asma go to the room to take a rest and Farzin are very relieved to see all this. She is happy in her heart that it is good that she did not have to do anything. She said to Shab as she goes.

"Shab as soon as possible, accept this reality! Anyway, I have heard that Shahzade Shazmaan does not give you as much attention as Riza gives me. Look where Shazmaan and where Shab! Now you will have to go back to Nikshahar, although it did not go well with you, maybe it is going right with Shahzade Shazmaan! In the true sense, Asma can prove to be the best companion for him. So get ready to get out of this palace. Good-Bye!" And Farzin also left from there.

As clouds of sorrow were raining on Shab one after the other, She could not understand why all this was happening to her and what was her fault that no one wants to see her here.

"I don't know when this time will pass out... I wish! I can leave for the Nikshahar today! In this palace, all are like-minded people...! I don't know what sin I did

And this is new trouble.....Sultana!" Shab said in his mind.

The Sahar came from the front; she was gasping and said to the princess Shab.

"Princess Shab, all your belongings have been thrown out of your room. I tried to stop valets repeatedly but they did not listen. Zan-e-Ardashir's sister has decided to stay in that room.

"But that room is mine! Did you inform Prince Shazmaan? Maybe all this happened with his permission. Without his permission, it is not possible. Why are they all doing this to me? As far as Sultana is concerned, she only wants to marry her sister to Shazmaan but I did not expect this from Shazmaan." Shab said.

"Princess Shab! At the moment, I must care of your

belongings from spoilage and put them in another room. Otherwise, some things may get spoiled." Sahar said.

"You go, I sending some valets to meet Prince Shazmaan for discussion about this. Shab said to Sahar and sent the message to the valets to have a meeting with prince Shazmaan. Prince Shazmaan sent back the message that he is in the garden with Hassan and he doesn't want to waste his precious time. Shab could not tolerate this and reached the garden where Shazmaan was with Hassan.

"Bebakhshid (I'm sorry)! ....I knew that you did not allow me to meet you, but the issue is such that I had to come,

"What's the matter?"

"My belongings from our room, the gifted clothes, and some essential things have been kept outside on the ground or to say that my belongings have been removed. And Asma has decided to stay in my room. What would have been the reason for doing this? Just want to know." Shab said.

"I think....Asma is our special guest and then it is only a matter of few days till that you can live comfortably in some other place. Shazmaan said.

"but that's your room too? all your things are in your room. As far as I know, it is wrong to get things out like this, without anyone's permission and then such treatment happens to slaves!" Shab said.

"That is my room! Any guest can stay there ... It is our duty to provide hospitality to our guests and you should also learn this. You can stay in some other place. I will not say anything more than this, you can go." Shazmaan said and left from there.

"Princess Shab! No room is empty. I searched all over the palace. There are few rooms but not special for a Princess.

And here I have got a place near the garden, but we can live there comfortably. Even the noise of the palace will not reach there and the valets are changing that place into your room. As you like roses, there are a lot of roses and a beautiful garden. There is a more relaxed feeling than the palace." Sahar said.

"Maybe this is what fate has approved," Shab said and went to her new room.

Chapter 10.

Shazmaan, Riza, and Ammu Baba were walking into the Garden and taking fresh air as a dose. After walking for a long time, Ammu Baba felt tired and sat down in the garden right in front of Shab's new room. Ammu Baba felt that the place is cleaned and a little changed. Ammu Baba asked Riza.

"Has any new valet come? It seems to be a very clean person, how beautiful flowers and fragrance is coming from …Nice!"

"No, I don't know, Baba! Maybe Shazmaan Dadash knows who is living here" said Riza.

"But I don't even know!" said Shazmaan.

Suddenly two white rabbits were running through the garden and sat at Riza's feet. The sound of someone's chortle was coming from the front. The face was not visible in the sunshine but she took a baby rabbit in her lap and white birds were flying around. The color of her dress was light pink and white. Hair was shining. Everyone started looking at her silently. Shazmaan got the same fragrance again.

"Maybe we are in a paradise….! What a lovely feeling and how much peace is there in the air, today. I have forgotten all the things…" Riza said to Ammu Baba.

"I feel that angels have come to pick me up…and I can see

them with our open eyes. But I cannot see the face of this angel…Shazmaan can you see who she is?"

"Baba…even I can't see her because of sunshine…so much peace around us. Means a lot of relaxation…." Shazmaan said.

Then the rabbit jumped up from her lap and started running and sat beside Shazmaan and Shazmaan picked it up in his lap.

"Where are you going, where is the little naughtier…!" Saying this, that voice stopped. Ammu Baba and Riza looked at Shab in surprise. Shazmaan didn't even blink.

"So that was you..?" Riza asked Shab.

"Excuse me! And Good Morning! Ammu Baba….."Shab said

"Good morning! My Child, have you also gone out for a walk?" Ammu Baba questioned Shab.

"No Ammu Baba! I was trying to play with these rabbits….When I woke up today, they were roaming in the garden and I too came out seeing them."

"For a moment I felt that today God had sent angels to call me." Saying this Ammu Baba started laughing loudly.

"Look, for this evening the feast has been arranged, rabbit meat…." Riza said with a laugh.

"Are you going to eat them, Prince Riza? Shab said cheerlessly.

"No, not at all… Riza is joking. Ammu Baba said.

"Thank God...!" Shab said slowly.

"Shab do you know who has come here? Don't know how long this place was useless and somewhat today its condition has changed. Ammu Baba asked Shab.

Shab looked at Shazmaan and then said to Ammu Baba.

"Sahar lives here, Baba! She gets tired of serving me… so she rests here".

Shazmaan stood silently and he understood that Shab is staying here and she has made an excuse of Sahar.

Ammu Baba gestured to Riza, "We think you have to talk to Shazmaan and we should go now. Khuda Hafiz!"

"Khuda Hafiz, Baba!"

Shazmaan leaves the rabbit on the ground and says to Shab "If I'm not wrong you are living here?"

"Baleh! (Yes)

"Safe place!"

"More than your room!"

"Well, you spell out good to Baba …just like this handle every issue, it would be better for you."

"This is wrong... if not today then tomorrow Baba will surely come to know about the truth. Shab said.

"Just keep doing what I'm telling you, it would be better for all of us….I don't love anything more than Baba and Riza…even if it is my own life."

There is waiting for me in the morning gathering and I cannot waste this time with you. It is my advice that you should not waste your time unnecessarily, on these baseless matters!" Shazmaan said to Shab and left from there.

"Self-indulgent man...!" Shab said.

Everyone was present in the Bazmgah (meeting room). Riza, Ammu Baba and Shazmaan, Farzin, Sultana, Hassan, Asma, except Shahzadi Shab. Ammu Baba was very happy to see this gathering. But his eyes were wandering here and there, again and again, was looking for Shab.

Sultana mentioned, "I'm glad that the Ezdevaaj of Zahedan's heir and Prince Shazmaan have been completed and that Sultan will soon be crowned. He has an unaccounted sultanate but I want it to continue. I want Shazmaan to get married to Asma."

Shazmaan, Riza, and Ammu Baba were surprised. It was not even a month for Ezdevaaj and they didn't know why such a thought came to her mind.
"I can't even imagine that…."Shazmaan said surprisingly.
"But it is a custom….. In Persia, every sultan has many wives. From whom many heirs are ruling the sultanate. You alone can't handle such a big sultanate. Zahedan is still without a sultan. And you are in Qasr-e-kand." Sultana insisted.

"You cannot decide what is going on in my life and what will happen. I'm happy with whatever I have and Zahedan was ours before and is still ours today and always will be, whether I rule it or Riza! You should take care of your sultanate. I am not one of those sly sultans who keep many wives or produce many heirs to get some fame. I dislike your Idea." Shazmaan said wrathfully.
"Baba, please convince Shazmaan," said Sultana
"Sultana! Shazmaan has done this marriage with ease. I think Shazmaan is right." Baba said.

"But he is unhappy with his first wife, that is why he has given the servant-room to Shab, and then if he does not want to do another marriage, then why did he give his room to Asma."Sultana's words have set Shazmaan's chest on fire. Shazmaan was not taking a look at Ammu Baba. Ammu Baba became inconsolable.

"Shazmaan, if you liked Asma, then why didn't you tell informed me? And gave a servant-room to Shab! Ammu Baba said so and left from there.

Sultana looked at Shazmaan viciously and smiled. Shazmaan went after Ammu Baba. Shazmaan could have asked Sultana to leave the palace if he wanted, but he respected Sultana. But there was something else in her mind.

Sultan started whispering with one of his men at the time of Shaman. Hassan was also present there during their conversation.
"Listen carefully ... when everyone is asleep ... there is a room in the garden of the palace, where Shazmaan's wife Shab is staying… you have to set a fire in her room. If the story of Shab is over, then our path will be completely clear. But be careful, no one can see you."
"As you say, be carefree."

Riza and Shazmaan went to Ammu Baba's room. Ammu Baba ignores Shazmaan and tells Riza.
"Today a loved one has attacked on our heart… on our hopes and also on our upbringing….!"
"Baba, don't be angry with me, I tell you the reality!" Shazmaan said
"I'll tell you the reality…. I know you don't love anyone but you can hold in esteem someone…. In the palace of Qasr-e-kand, the elder prince Shazmaan's wife is living in a servant's room and there is someone else in your room. And this is a matter of shame. In a few days, this news will spread to the whole city. Your father loved your mother so much. It is our family tradition that we should respect our

companions. Two souls make life a journey and together they make the difficulties easier. Unless you understand each other, you cannot understand the importance of each other. I'm also angry with Shab. They supported you but on the wrong issue." Baba explained Shazmaan.

"But I do not go to my room myself and I did not even know that Shab left the palace and staying in servant-room… Sultana and Asma might have liked my room so I did not stop them…. Shazmaan said in hurriedness.

"So it's clear that you want to separate Shab forever from yourself?" Riza said.

Then one of the servants of the palace said to Shazmaan in haste.

"Sir, There is a horrible fire in the room of Shahzadi Shab……the door is locked….tried to open it but could not succeed."

Riza, Baba, and Shazmaan reached the accident site as soon as possible and order the servants of the palace to pour water. The place was completely burnt. There was only smoke of ashes everywhere. But no sound came from there. It was a coincidence that Shab was not present there and Sahar was busy with the work of the palace.

"Shab...!" Ammu Baba's condition started deteriorating as soon as he said this. Baba felt that perhaps Shab was no more. After hearing the noise, Shab came running fast towards her room.

Shab got scared, seeing her belongings turned to ashes, she stood silently. Nothing came out of her tongue.

"How did all this happen ...? There was no such thing in my room, which could be used to start a fire. Then who would have done all this?" Baba, what is all this happening with me ever since I came here, nothing is going right... today my stuff is burnt, tomorrow I'm too Shab became so sad that it was difficult to handle her.

"Whoever did this act must not have gone far from the palace... Riza asked permission from Shazmaan and he went out for an investigation with the soldiers, they got strict restrictions in the palace and garden.

During the investigation, a soldier saw a shadow in the corner of the garden. When he followed that shadow, his leg got staggered by something. Looking through the flambeau, there was Hassan who was breathing deeply. The soldier made a noise and called Riza, Shazmaan. Shazmaan lifted Hassan in his lap.

"Hassan my dear... what happened to you.... Shazmaan asked Hassan.

"Ameh (Khala or Aunt)...Shab...Killed..." Hassan's hand fell to the ground as soon as he said this. Hassan is no more.

"Hassan... please get up and say something... Hassan!" Shazmaan kept talking.

"Hassan has a mark on his face..." said Riza.

"Whoever has done this Riza? He should feel the same pain....he should have the same condition Riza...the murderer should be presented in front of us as soon as possible....now I can't tolerate it!" Shazmaan ordered Riza. The murderer could not run very far. A soldier caught the murderer climbing the wall of the palace and presented him in front of prince Shazmaan. At the same time, Sultana also came there and started crying loudly on seeing Hassan.

Shazmaan asked the murderer, "Who are you and how did you come to the palace... why did you kill this child..... Speak quickly before beheading you."

"My Lord! I did not kill this child. Shahzadi Shab had called me to the palace and ordered me to set fire to her room.
Hassan was playing in the garden and he had listened to us, due to which the princess Shab held his breath...so Hassan can't tell you about this conspiracy...I also appealed to her...that Leave Hassan...but she ordered me to leave the palace..." the murderer explained.

"You are lying...I don't even know you...and why would I kill Hassan...and burn my room... have some fear to God..." Shab said.
"Hassan took your name in his last breath...I want to know why you did this.... Shazmaan said to Shab.
"Trust us, we have not done anything and we do not even know this person....who is he from where...and why does he want to trap us. Shab said crying
"If we are lying, did you come to the garden or not.... said the man
"Yes...I came but..."
Sultana interrupted Shab in the middle.
"It's enough... now everything has been revealed in front of everyone...how did you even think about such a big crime...did you not even have mercy on this little life.... Prince Shazmaan! Is this your justice...? The murderer is in front of you, still, you are waiting...that he should kill us too...I need revenge for Hassan."

"But I didn't do anything... Baba, believe me." Shab said to Ammu Baba.

"I was sure......but..." Saying this Baba fell silent.

"Baba .....? Riza....please you believe me...I can't do all this...that I can never take someone's life......Trust me for God's sake....." Shab started weeping but no one wanted to hear anything.

"It's too much....and how much will you demean yourself ....what was the fault of this little life...you know Baba was praising you right now....Baba, she is your Shab...and this is her reality...she didn't accept that Asma and Jan-e-Ardashir (wife of Ardashir) should stay here....and that's why she cheated us..." Shazmaan said angrily.

"But please let me explain myself....Give me a chance to present my explanation of innocence..." Shab tried to speak and then Sultana came to dominate Shazmaan.

"Damn it all Shazmaan! on your justice....you are still thinking...She should also be given the death penalty.... Sultana said.

"No...I will first give her a chance to prove her innocence. If she is found guilty, she will be given a death sentence...I will kill her daily... Will make her realize her guilt every day..." Shazmaan went through the roof.

"Please, believe me, I am guilt-less...I didn't do anything" Shab said.

"I declare that Shab will have to live as a slave for twenty days. In the meantime, she will be given only one chance to prove herself innocent. Exactly after twenty days, she will be given the death penalty. Till that time she will be under house arrest. And now she is just a slave."

Shab did not have any bed or anything special to eat. Shab's goods had already been burnt in the fire. Shab was cursing her fate every day by sleeping on a stone pillow. After three days she wanted to go to Nikshahar but fate imprisoned her here. Sometimes she missed her Sultan Naveed very much. Surely Sultan Naveed would trust her but four days passed, and Sultan Naveed didn't come.

Shab says to Sahar, "Look, this is the result of this Ezdevaaj. Dadash (brother) did not come because he also thinks that I am guilty. From the first day, I knew that no one cares for me. This world becomes my enemy unnecessarily.

Shazmaan had put Shab under house arrest, so even Sahar could not meet her. Shab did everything that a slave does. If she felt hungry after doing heavy work, she would have had the good fortune to eat only one time. Shab became weak. Ammu Baba can't see her condition.

"My heart says you are innocent but….all the evidence is against you." Ammu Baba said to Shab.

"Ammu Baba that day…Hassan was calling me…that…Shab Ameh you will be killed by fire…I felt strange why someone wanted to kill me…I came out of the room. I didn't see Hassan… just following his voice I was going and I reached the garden. I also called Hassan after that, his voice did not come then I heard the noise that my room is on fire and I started running fast here and by then all my belongings were burnt. Baba, it was not my fault, I am telling the truth. Even I didn't know that person." Shab said.

Shazmaan was passing by when she said to Ammu Baba.
"Baba, you are here? you must be explained. Talking to slaves is against your principles… and a slave who is a criminal!! Shazmaan said looking at Shab.
"Shazmaan I feel that this matter should be investigated one more time. For my satisfaction." Ammu Baba said
"Baba, I want to tell you something. Whatever happened to Sultan Ardashir and Sultana is a very sad matter. Ardashir will never forgive me and I cannot forgive myself either. Sultana wants me to marry Asma anyway. Even now I have nothing to do with this slave..... And perhaps by doing this I can save myself from the woe of Ardashir." Shazmaan said.

"Do whatever you want, but before that ask that person again just for me… only once but strictly. After that do whatever comes to your heart. This time I will not stop you. I must walk. Khuda Hafiz!" Ammu Baba leaves from there. Shazmaan looks at Shab differently.
"By tomorrow clean this garden, it is your responsibility to take special care of cleanliness. Twenty-five baskets of dry fruits ... to be delivered safely from the meeting hall. Before that, the palace has to be brightened like a mirror, remember this work cannot be done by someone, and you will do this work alone, After that, you clean my room and present special dishes for me during the evening. Anyway, there are only a few days left in your life, till then I will remind you every day what you have done. The special thing is whether you are a slave in the palace or that person, so I want you to bring at least thirty jugs from the well of Qasr-e-kand." Shazmaan ordered Shab.

Shab said to Shazmaan, 'But it must have taken a lot of time to bring water from the well of Qasr-e-kand. The rest of the work will not be completed even at the time of evening."

"You should care about this, not me....if this doesn't finish, then whatever you are getting this time, will not be destined even for one time."

"It is too much Dadash (brother), no one does this even to his enemy..." suddenly Riza came there.

"Riza! It is too little for her…. Shazmaan said.

Saying this Shazmaan and Riza left from there.

Chapter 11.

About ten days passed. Only some time was left, showing his intelligence, Riza investigated the matter thoroughly and told Shazmaan.

"Dadash, I have to talk to you in private… the matter is different, if you give permission, then I want to discuss this matter in Bazmgah (meeting Hall). Riza and Shazmaan went to Bazmgah.

"Say!"

"Dadash do you remember when Shahzadi Shab's room caught fire…there was a lot of noise there, everyone was present but Sultana wasn't present there and that person can't even speak our language properly. I asked him strictly then he was saying something in Arabic. I have called an Interpreter who knows many languages. I have full doubts about Sultana." Riza said.

"But why would Sultana do this..?" Shazmaan asked.

The soldier and interpreter came and told Shazmaan something that was going to change Shab's life.

The soldier did a thorough investigation of that Arab man and the interpreter asked him the reason for his coming here.

"Salam, Prince Shazmaan! ....this person is Sultana's man and that was Sultana who had called him here. He said that Sultana wanted to get Shahzadi Shab killed so that Asma could get her place. Hassan was present there at that time and listened to everything. They thought that Shab was in her room and threw the flambeau inside. At that very moment, Shab must have heard Hassan's voice and by coincidence, she was saved. While this man and sultana were running away, they saw Hassan there and Sultana too. Sultana was trying to keep Hassan quiet and Sultana placed a hand on Hassan's face due to which he started having trouble breathing and finally he stopped breathing.

 "Oh God, what kind of atrocity is this? Riza Sultana and Asma should be presented here." Shazmaan said in sorrow.
"It is hard to say that she has gone from here overnight… or to say that she has escaped," Riza informed.

 "This man should be imprisoned forever. Riza….Thanks for your hard work on this….Hassan was dear to me and I will regret it forever." Shazmaan said.
"Dadash, I feel that at this time we should apologize to Shahzadi Shab. Riza said.
"Riza…I'm not able to contact her.….Riza I realize I've done a lot wrong with her. I have insulted her most of all. In such a situation, it will not be right for me to talk to her. I gave her a lot of pain." Shazmaan said while embarrassing.
"You are right, but at this time free her from your detention…her condition is not good… let's go Dadash! Also gives this news to Ammu Baba. He was also worried about Shab. Now, Baba will also be fine." Riza said.

Riza along with Ammu Baba and Shazmaan goes to Shab. Shab used to clean the palace gardens at that time and sometimes she would sit again tired. Shab's face was already weak. Her body had become very thin. Riza and Shazmaan could not speak due to embarrassment. Ammu Baba placed his hand on the tired Shab's head and said, "Wake up my Child! It is enough now. God has accepted our prayers. You are now free from this slavery. You had faith in God... and God kept his mercy on you...Your truth opened everyone's eyes."

"Is it so Baba? I'm free now. There was different happiness on Shab's face.
"Baleh!" Ammu Baba said
"I wanted to be free and God listened to me. Baba, I want to be free from every restriction that compels me to live here. Shab said
"I didn't get you Shab..." Baba said.

"When I was a slave, I used to think that the day I became free, I would walk away from you all, So far so that you all do not bother to see my face again and I think I shouldn't waste so much time. I have to leave with Sahar." Shab explained to Baba.

"But we all want to apologize to you...we all have a misunderstanding...give us a chance..." said Riza.
"What's the matter of apology...if someone else was in your place; he would have done the same thing. But before resolving any issue, it is very important to hear from both sides so that no one gets hurt before taking a decision. One should handle the sultanate in the same way. The real

Sultan is also the one who first listens to everyone... then declares his own decision... Is it right, Baba?" Shab said.

"Of course… because of this ability and understanding, I've chosen you as Shazmaan's companion. You have the strength to tolerate, even after so much, I remained silent so that Shazmaan himself should learn from his experience…It is my fault too that I could not stop all this from happening. I also want to apologize to you." Ammu Baba said.

"No Ammu Baba…you are embarrassing me…just allow me to leave…."Shab asked.
"I feel that Shazmaan and Shab should talk for once. Come on, Riza, this is the life of these two, now they should decide whether they want to live together or not. Saying this Baba and Riza left from there.

For a long time, It was silence there.

Shazmaan says to Shab.
"I'm very sorry for what happened…I shouldn't do that."

Hearing this, Shab leaves from there. Shab ignores Shazmaan and Shazmaan stood silently. Here Shab said a lot to Shazmaan without saying anything. Words were not needed but Shab's neglect left an impression on his heart and mind like he is not necessary for her.

Shab goes to the palace and meets Sahar and asks Sahar to leave the palace and left from there. Sahar was happy to see Shab and agrees to walk. Shab tells Sahar that she doesn't want to go to Nikshahar. She wants to go away somewhere else where there is neither Sultan Naveed nor

Shazmaan. Shab also wants to go away from their reach. Now she will live her life alone. Her relationship with everyone is broken. At this time Sahar expresses her displeasure. She was a maidservant, who can work only in the palace. She could only serve a princess in the palace, nothing more than that. At this Shab says to Sahar, "I'm used to this…..if you also leave me alone, It wouldn't affect me." Shab said sadly.

Shab did not take any time to leave the palace. Shab had covered a long-distance journey. It was a bit difficult but not impossible. Shab knew how to ride, so there was no problem. She kept on fixing her journey towards the direction of the ocean.

The darkness was killing the light. Where will Shab go alone? Doesn't she feel afraid? No, Shab had spent many nights alone in the palace as a slave. At that time she was not aware of hunger and thirst. Many times she cursed herself, "I wish! May death take me into its lap!" God is playing so many games. First parents left her, then Farzin's Maman, and then Shazmaan. Then Sultan Naveed betrayed her with great love. God bless them with all this kind of wealth. At least Shab is free and Sahar whom she never considered a maidservant, she also left Shab alone. Now only God will show a path. Whatever happened was God's will. If God gave sorrow, then God will also give them strength to bear the sorrow.

After traveling a long journey, Shab stops at one place, she feels very hungry and thirsty too. The place was as if a market is held here every day, but due to a long delay, the market had started closing. She cloaked herself in black and had made a niqab on her face. Nearby, a younger fruit-seller was packing his shop. Shab was very hungry, maybe a pomegranate will work. Thirst will also be quenched. Thinking that Shab went to that Fruit-seller. Shab said to Mevdaar (fruit-seller).

"Can I have a pomegranate?"
"Of course! You can madam, but after paying its price and you will get it at less price because by tomorrow it would be rot. Tell me how much you want?"
"Just one, but I have nothing to pay for…Can you give this to me for free? Shab asked.

"Ohh my God! what kind of oppression is it? It seems that my life will be spent feeding everyone for free. Don't know who gives my address to these people. Everyone wants to take advantage of my generosity. Well, take pomegranate and this melon too! But again I will not give you anything for free." Fruit-seller overreacted.

"Merciful soul! (Very kind)"Shab said.
Then the old lady comes there and tells Mevdaar.
"It's been a long time, Mohsin! Now let's...,
"Just coming! Maman There is only a little work left. Fruit-seller replied.
Maman saw Shab and questioned Shab.
"Who are you and what are you doing here so late? It is dark; you should not leave your home like this. There are more than enough scoundrels who can kidnap you and later sell you to distant countries. I believe that you should not be here at this time. What kind of your relatives are? Who left you here?"

Shab said, "I'm alone and I have no one. I want to go near the ocean but it is too late at night." On hearing this, the elderly woman hold Shab's hand and took her to the tenement, and lift Shab's niqab from her face.

"You speak like royal family… you must be princess… or the servant of some princess...no one interacted me in this kind of sweet words before....who are you? Before that fruit-seller comes, tell me the truth!"The elderly woman asked.

Then Mohsin came there and asked about Shab to Maman, "Maman do you know who she is?"

"She is my daughter and she has come to pick me up from here! Say something, my child. Maman, blinking, pointed towards Shab.

"...Baleh...!" Shab said.

"…Ah God finally eased my troubles. What kind of daughter you are? You left an old woman on a way… do you have some embarrassment!" Just then Maman stops Mohsin and asks them to sleep at his owner's house tonight. Mohsin agrees and he asks the elderly lady to take care of her and leaves from there.

Shab was surprised that what is the matter and what is happening all. Did Shab come to the wrong place? There was fear in Shab's heart. The eyes of that elderly woman were turquoise, just like Shazmaan's. And face a glimpse like Riza. But Shab had never seen Shazmaan's family so it was difficult to think so.

"Something must have happened to you… or else no one can leave their home like this. You have jewelry on your neck and a ring on your finger, it means you are married,

have your husband left you…?”
The old woman asked.

 “Yes, he left me…and I too…he loves his people, kingdom more than me”. Shab replied.
"People...? So you're a princess... what's your prince's name? Old Woman asked.
“Shazmaan…the future Sultan of Zahedan…!” Shab said.
Hearing this, there was no limit to the happiness of Maman and her eyes became open, she again asked Shab, "Is Shazmaan safe and Riza too? And where do they both live? Will you introduce me to them...they are my soul...you know how many years I've been looking for them...just once... Let's take it...I am their Maman....and I went to Zahedan to meet them but I didn't find anyone there... since then I am in search of them... our physical condition was not good... Because of this, I'm not able to meet them...you introduce me to them...” The Maman said pleading with Shab.

Hearing this, there was no limit to the happiness of Maman and his eyes became open, he again asked Shab, "Is Shazmaan safe and Riza too? And where do they both live? Will you introduce me to them...they are my soul...you know how many years I've been looking for them...just once... Let's take it...I am their Maman....and I went to Zahedan to meet him but I didn't find anyone there... since then I am in search of them... our physical condition was not good... Because of this, I'm not able to meet them...you introduce me to them...” The Maman said pleading with Shab.

Shab was surprised. Shab asked, "What? Are you Shazmaan's mother? And how did you get this condition and how can you say that you are Shazmaan's mother?"

 "Shazmaan will surely recognize me…Please introduce me to them." The old woman said.

"I will get it done but before that, please tell me how you parted with Shazmaan and Riza? And what happened to the Sultan?"

"That night….Sultan Mahvish heard strange noises…and he went out to look. Riza was in my lap and Shazmaan was sleeping. Sultan Mahvish did not return as soon as he left the palace… And that sound stopped… I was nervous. I asked Sultan's younger brother Behrouz to take care of Shazmaan and Riza and I came out of the palace in search of Sultan Mahvish…The search was on…Some creepy eyes, in some dark-colored clothes, were looking at me.

They had killed Mahvish Sultan….as soon as I tried to yell; they put their hands on my face and kidnapped me. I fainted…when I opened my eyes, I was somewhere else…many women like me were present in one room.

Every day, those predators sold a woman to another country. Some of them were princesses and some were common women. I wanted to escape for my Shazmaan and Riza. I tried a lot … to escape from this ban but in the end, when the time came to sell me, they took me to the ship.

There were other women with me. I knew how to swim and from one corner I jumped from the ship into the river….and they all thought I committed suicide….after that, I started looking for my children like a lunatic for many years.

I made my condition like a beggar and started begging so that I could visit Zahedan. And when I reached Zahedan there was no one there. I thought maybe Shazmaan and Riza have been killed too. When I asked some people about them, then it came to know that Behrouz had taken them somewhere far away from where no one was aware of it.

Since then I am looking for them but don't know where my sons are? You are Shazmaan's companion...please I want to meet him once." said the old woman.

 "Will your sons recognize you? If not then what will you do?" Shab asked.

"They'll recognize me for sure...!" said the old woman.
"So it's decided that I will try to introduce you to them but promise me that you will not mention me to them," Shab said.
"Promise, Sweet Child!" said the old woman.
For a while, the Maman kept looking at Shab. Maman could not control herself and she asked Shab.
"Doesn't Shazmaan love you...? Or you don't like him...? Tell me something about yourself too. Which country's princess are you?"

 "I don't know Maman… even I'm not a princess… I am just an orphan and nothing else." Shab said.
"It's so sad....alright! You also call yourself an orphan and to me Maman also!" Maman said, placing her hand on Shab's head.

"…Look how God connects one person to another…..
Connects the strings of human beings….and teaches
human beings to respect each other. The need and
importance of each other become known automatically.
You are very sad...something must have happened to
you...because of that you left everything...and came so far
away. Didn't even care that there are so many people in the
outside world who just want to take advantage of a woman
by seeing her alone. If we weren't here today, you probably
wouldn't be here too."

"Maman, I have been cheated from a young age… and
now I do not have enough strength to be deceived again. I
do not like this life… I just want to be free and alone. It's
better to be alone than to live with cheaters."Shab
mentioned.

Chapter 12.

Today the palace was somewhat silent. There was no movement of any kind. The morning was as usual. Today, Ammu Baba did not come out of his room for a walk. Riza went to Ammu Baba and Asked about his condition and later went to Shazmaan's room. Shazmaan was not present there. Riza went to find him in the garden. Shazmaan was alone in the room where Shab lived which was burnt later. Riza found Shazmaan a little sad. The room smelled of wine. There were cups and jugs everywhere in the room. Riza understood.

"Good morning, Dadash…! Since when did you start all this. You were not like that…it is not good for health." Riza said.

Shazmaan looked at Riza. Blue eyes were red and tired too. Shazmaan said to Riza, "The whole night was spent searching for Shab but she could not be found. Wanted to apologize to her and I also went to Nikshahar. Shab was not found there too. I talked to Sahar. Sahar told that she did not know where she had gone….Riza! Is Shab?" Shazmaan stopped.

"Dadash you care so much about the Shab…I am surprised… No Dadash, don't mislead me. You have no relation with Shab and even if she becomes dear to God, It doesn't matter to you! You only care about me and Baba, no one else."

"It's enough Riza...I know that It was my mistake...but pray that wherever Shab is, she should be safe!" Shazmaan said displeasure.

"You are turning...Dadash! Today, I am glad to see that you are worrying about Shab to whom you were not accepting." Riza said.

"Riza Shab is a different one... Despite being a princess, she converted the room of a servant into her room. Tolerated my ignorance and despite being innocent, she completed her sentence. ...she didn't disobey me and kept doing as I ordered her...she didn't think even once about her happiness...if she wanted, she could have insisted but not...she accepted every my decision because..."

"Because the princess considers you as her world...just a means of living...and I want that the reason for your living should be the same...not everyone gets love and you are lucky... that you have princess Shab ... otherwise, look at Farzin, she doesn't think anything is important except beautiful clothes, nuts to eat, and comfort." Saying this, Riza and Shazmaan started laughing. Shazmaan hugged Riza.

"For your kind information, let me tell you that the princess Shab has taken your royal horse...The princess does not know that your royal ride is something special..." said Riza.

"And our ass ride must be waiting for us outside, now we should not waste much time….So now we should go towards our destination."

Shazmaan said and looked out from the door of the palace, his ride was ready there. This ride was special because it remembered the way of the journey. It understood his master very well Shazmaan.

Shazmaan said to his royal horse.
"Come on friend! Where did you take princess? In no time, his speed increased. Shazmaan reached that market, tearing the wind.
There were a lot of crowds and seeing the royal ride, everyone was making a way for Shazmaan. Shazmaan got down from his ride. He said again, "Friend, point me where you left her, and Shazmaan's ride stopped exactly in front of the Mohsin's shop. Shazmaan understood. He asked Mevdaar (Fruit-Seller), "Listen….Can you help me?"

"Your Highness! Tell me what you want to take…?" Mohsin said.
"Yesterday a lady came here…I just want to know about her."
"Your Highness! Many women come here… for who, are you talking about? I think you are talking about her who yesterday came here to meet her Maman (Mother)? I know her sir…I'm calling her right now."

Mohsin went to his tenant and told the elderly Maman and Shab that a prince has come outside. On the other hand, Shazmaan was surprised that Shab's Maman is also there. Elderly Maman comes out and Shab looks out from the window of the tenant... Shab wondered how Shazmaan had come here, how did he know that Shab was there. But Shab was happy for Maman that the person she was looking for was himself in front of her.

"Who are you...?" Maman asked to Shazmaan.
"I am Shazmaan....and...!" As Shazmaan said, Maman caressed his face and started looking at him again and again, sometimes in his hands in his eyes, and Maman broke down.
"The same...eye, Shazmaan! I am your mother...look at me!

"Maman? Who are you? Everyone knows that I lost my mother in childhood. But how can you say that you are my Mother? Shazmaan asked confusedly.

"My child! Look at me carefully....Your father's name was Mahvish and Behrouz who is your Ammu...and Riza my little Son!"

"But how can I believe? Everyone knows that..."

"Let me remind you, that you will of surety believe me. Do you remember that night when your Father and Mother lost from the Palace? You know what happened that night. Your father was killed that night and you were sleeping. I handed over Riza to Behrouz and when I went to search the Sultan, there was his dead body and before I could give any voice to anyone...they kidnapped me....that night you promised the Sultan that you will keep Zahedan safe and will never allow any kind of trouble to come in his land... Hearing this, the Sultan took you in his lap. Your father always used to tell you that always keep calm as the moon and keep lustrous like it. Do you

remember or have you forgotten this too?"
For a moment there was a silence. Shazmaan was looking into the eyes of Maman.

"And you love white birds too! Do you remember that line which we used to encore together?" Maman asked.

"These white birds are the symbol of peace."
Shazmaan and Maman encored this line.

"I'm sorry Maman! ...I remember and I'm convinced that you are my mother...only me, Baba and you knew this special thing and Riza was very young at that time so he didn't even know.... Shazmaan's eyes came with tears while saying this. Maman hugged Shazmaan.
Mohsin was surprised that he had been taken care of Zahedan's Mallika. Shab was watching all this from the window and her eyes were also moist. Maman wanted to call Shab but was compelled by her promise and she didn't even want to leave Shab alone.

"For so many years I was in this dilemma, not knowing what would have happened that night! Maman, I was out in search of someone special today, but I found you even more special than that. It seems like some kind of miracle." Shazmaan said.

"Who is special... must be an angel... because I have met you today...
Must be God's good heart person ...will you tell me who is that person?" Maman asked Shazmaan.

"I will tell you but before that I want you to go to the palace....and meet Riza...he didn't even see you but today

Riza will be very happy…hey boy! Listen you can come with us". Shazmaan said to Mohsin.

"But, what about maman's Daughter?" Mohsin asked.
The promise of Maman and Shab has been fulfilled but here Shab has been missed. Shazmaan knew that Shab is here but he showed that he does not know anything and asked Mohsin to prepare a good and safe ride.

He also left a letter for Riza. Shazmaan knew that Ammu Baba would recognize Maman and Mohsin would carefully take Maman to the palace.
Everyone gets ready to go to the palace and Shazmaan pretends that he is also going with them. So that Shab does not suspect that Shazmaan didn't go. Shab was disappointed at Maman's departure and was also afraid that she was here alone in this tenant, lest the owner of the fruit-seller asks her to vacate that place.

Maman and Mohsin left.
Shab sat silent like this. Evening's time was about to come. Shab closed the door and lit the lamp placed in front of her. Shab was sitting with her face, placed in her hands, and was watching the passers-by as they came. But Shab was silent. Shab was remembering her childhood that she wished she would get her Maman and Baba in the same way.
They also loved Shab so much. But Shab had seen them, their corpse! at that time Shab was a little child around 6 and she remembers it too.
That was a dreadful scene....the ship of the ocean was sunk and in that ship, there were Maman and Baba of Shab.

Shab wanted to go near the ocean and wanted to ask about the ocean lot. Shab was in deep thought.

There was a door on the roof in that tenant from which one could easily enter the tenant and Shazmaan came in through the step ladder which was built inside the door. Shazmaan sat down near Shab with his silent feet and kept some dry fruits to eat and a jug of water near Shab. Shab had no idea that Shazmaan was sitting near her. Shazmaan kept looking at Shab for a long time. Don't know what Shab is thinking? Shazmaan made a slight noise. Shab saw it ... and when Shab looked again, Shab screamed out panicky.

"Oh, My God!" Shab's heartbeat had increased and she was very nervous. Shab remained like this for some time. "I'm sorry princess...! I shouldn't have scared you like this...Look what I've got for you." Shazmaan said.

"How did you come in, I had closed the door... and who scares like this. You had gone with Maman." Shab asked. "Calm Down! Princess ...I came from the roof!" "But, why you come here?"

"I have come to take you back to the palace...!" Shazmaan told Shab It was almost midnight and Shazmaan and Shab were silent. Shab neither ate anything nor looked towards Shazmaan.

"Whatever happened ...it happened unintentionally...I didn't want to hurt you. I'm ashamed of what I did. ... I could not take the right decision in a hurry. Hassan was very dear to me..! His death made me incapable of seeing and hearing anything else." Shazmaan said.

Shazmaan knew that Shab was very angry and it was difficult for Shazmaan to overcome Shab's displeasure. But Shazmaan had something else in her mind.
Shab got up and started looking outside the window.
"Maybe you don't like my presence…. Since when only I'm talking, you're not speaking a single word!"
"You shouldn't have been here. Shab said while looking into Shazmaan's eyes.

"The Sultan of Zahedan… should not be with any other woman. What will your people say… and your wife would also worry about you." Shab's tone was different. Shazmaan was surprised at Shab's words and was looking at Shab very differently.

"Another woman...? Who is another woman Shab? And what are you saying about all this? …you are my wife and you are my companion."

"You are bothering me a lot. And what are you saying…? You had said that day …that… you had made me your companion because you did not want to disobey Baba and… you do not care for anyone. I'm still a slave to you and there is no relation with me. What I have suffered since childhood, you will not even realize it for the rest of your life.
I also had a sultanate…I also had people, but I handed them all over for the happiness of my family.

Everyone just took advantage of me…..but when our marriage decided with you, I felt that you would listen to me, talk a lot to me….but you made me feel like I'm spoiling your pride. I did not expect anyone in the world that someone can love me. My parents passed away in childhood. Farzin's mother never loved me. Farzin only hates me. I wanted the love of my Maman and Baba but unfortunately, I didn't get it.

Sahar and Naveed Dadash said that there can be no one better than Shazmaan for me but, they were wrong. Even the slaves were not treated the way I was treated. Just for water. It looked like the most dreadful night I spent as a punishment.

There was only darkness everywhere. You punished me without explaining myself. The sultans of these big palaces have a very small heart ...Of course very small. I knew that you dislike me and believed it when you gave my room to Asma. If you only liked Asma then why did you marry me??

These words coming out of Shab's tongue were emptying her heart.
"Shab..."
"Nah (no)… Prince Shazmaan, I also love my life as much as you love Riza and Baba. You are here today because you are sympathetic to me, and the reason you have got your mom. You got the reality of Hassan's death and Riza's happiness. You did not want to upset Baba, his happiness. But it was not my fault, I was also yours. But you have proved that no one is more selfish than you." Shab's eyes turned red… the tears were not stopping. As if someone had instigated the fire. Shazmaan thought it appropriate to remain silent. He wanted to hear Shab.

"I don't need Prince Shazmaan in my life….No need for anyone, I will spend my life alone….What was my fault? I remembered… my habit of worrying, living in simplicity, being loyal to everyone… all these made me guilty."

"So you have decided…then listen to my verdict…I will be with you till the last breath. Only with you….You probably think that I married Asma…but it's not true…I know I was something else earlier but I promise you that the Sultan of Zahedan will have only one Mallika…Shab and only Shab"

"You are making fun of me? So I should walk away from here….so far… that I never have to face you in life. I can't trust you in the slightest."

"Wherever you go I will find you…I'm not making fun of you….Understand It as the beginning of our love…."

"Whatever you say…no matter how hard you try…now I will never be able to trust you…Never… Even if I meet by coincidence, I will keep more distance from you…will go so far that only my name will remain…."
"This is your stubbornness…and you are very angry rights now…don't make such big claims. One day it will also happen that you will be involved in my love. I'll also be waiting for that day…" Shazmaan said.

"I can only laugh after hearing these! One who does not know how to make a better decision, how could be a better companion". Shab said.

Shazmaan was listening comfortably to everything because the words of Shab were not as painful as Shab's Past was.

Chapter 13.

"You knew that Hassan was the dearest to me and you brought him to death. What is going on in your mind now…? I want to know if you don't want to create any new trouble again." Ardashir asked dispiritedly.

'No....we will not give up my final cause in the middle...I will destroy them. Whoever goes against it, I will also give the death sentence...I just want my rule, only mine!" Sultana said while losing control herself.

"Sultana, I don't have that much power to go back to the battlefield... I am old now... and I have lost my dear Hassan… What kind of Justice is this? What is the need to punish an innocent person unnecessarily? The people of Zahedan are decent...don't commit your atrocities on them." Ardashir said to Sultana.

"You don't need to do anything... Your descendant will rule over the Zahedan and that's what I want…"

"Don't know why there is so much hatred and jealousy in your heart...we are not like your people at all. We know how to value humanity. We know how to live together...We have only love and love in our hearts and nothing. I'm well aware of what you did in Qasr-e-kand. Give up your stubbornness."Ardashir advised the Sultana.

Sultana sent her spies to Qasr-e-kand. She used to get the news of every city in five days. Due to Shab's precaution, Sultana could not know where Shab and Shazmaan were. Shab left the tenant's room silently the very next day.

When Shazmaan wakes up from his sleep, he feels very sad. This time his royal ride was not used by Shab.
On the same day, a message is sent to Shazmaan to return to the palace, but Shazmaan wanted to find Shab. This process continued for four days. This action of Shab was disturbing Shazmaan.

Shab had left for another city. The name of that city was Vashnam-e-Dari. Shab was staying there with her Maman's friend Arsya. Arsya was the maid-servant of Shab's mother but later she proved to be her best friend.
She had no child. The husband was a soldier in a distant Sultanate who died in the battle. Shab narrated her entire story to Arsya. She felt very sad. Now Shab started living there. Shab often made some maps in the night's peace and a book which aroused great excitement in Shab's heart to learn the Hindi language. Her interest grew and she started reading books. She wanted that she must go to Hind once. And in this thought, she forgot everything.
Shab often used to visit near the ocean. She liked the ocean very much. Meanwhile, she had forgotten that she was a princess and she had started living in simplicity. Now she liked loneliness because there was peace.

One day Arsya said to Shab.

"Now it is difficult for women to come out of their homes… Women are missing in the city. Some people say that women are being sold to other countries, especially young women……and the buyer is ready to pay a handsome price for those women… from which the people of the country are kidnapping and selling young women. The Sultan of our country is sitting with their eyes closed…"

"This is wrong...does no sultan want to decide on this? Khaleh Shazmaan's Maman also told me the same thing. Don't know... Since then, how many women were forced to hand over their self-esteem to others? I wish! I could have done something for all of them."

Shab wanted to get to the depth of it. Shab asked Arsya for the help of some informers who have excellent espionage skills. After a few days, Shab met Abtin and Anosh. Both were experts in espionage. Shab asked them to inquire about the daily missing happening in the country. Shab started getting all kinds of news. Now Shab has made it the purpose of her life. Innocent women will not have to be forced anymore. Their life should not be wasted like this.

Shazmaan was very upset for not getting Shab and went back to Qasr-e-kand. But Shazmaan had not changed his decision. He will get Shab tomorrow if not today. He had hope and he would never give up this hope. On reaching the palace, Shazmaan met Riza. Riza was very happy and he talked about Maman to Shazmaan. Riza was very happy to get Maman. But Shazmaan's face was sad. Riza asked him.

"Dadash, you are looking a bit troubled….my I know the reason for this, and, what about the princess Shab…? Didn't you take her with you?" Riza asked.

Shazmaan told everything to Riza. On this Riza gave an idea to Shazmaan.

"Till she was with you… you ignored her… and when you want her, she changed her way. Well, let me tell you a trick. You have a lot of informers and spies and I have too. And put them in search of Shab. Trust me, you will find Shab." Riza consoled.

"You're so kind! Thanks, Riza"
"Before it, you had said that you do not believe in love and today you have followed the same path. For years you were looking for Maman and Baba or you were looking for the reason where our parents are but today you are only looking for Shab and want her."

"I got everything without asking God, and now only Shab is needed…it seems as if…I don't exist without her." Shazmaan said.

"Don't worry… God will listen to you and …I will pray for you that you meet princess Shab." Riza said.
Many days passed like this. Shazmaan's hope was getting weak. Every day the informers just get failure.

On the other hand, Shab started getting busy with her motive. Shab could not remember that she also had a world where Maman, Riza, and Baba were there, and Shazmaan too. Shab's spies told that they had seen some ships that always remained on the banks of Chabahar at night. They come... some stuff happens and they have seen some women too.

"We need a Malon (shipman) who can direct that ship towards Hind…and he should be trustworthy. And for this task, I want to choose Abtin and Anosh. You both have to update me on every single news. Precaution is very important...yourself as well as that of the women who will be taken away."

Remember that no one should be harmed in this. Even before reaching Hind, free those women from captivity and send them to another ship, but there should be some other way so that no one can doubt. Then return those women to their families. I want this issue to be mentioned with all the Sultans of the country. But now the most important thing is the life of those women... So are you ready to help me?" Shab said.

"Baleh...always...!" said the detectives.

 "I will send you the map but this work should be done soon. I have a special book in which a place can be reached on the edge of Hind. The road is plain and hilly but those women will be in the ship and they can be saved only through the ship."
'You're right...! We will surely succeed in our motive.... Khuda Haffiz!"
"Khuda Haffiz...!" Shab said.

Shab was successful and she was glad that God had chosen her for this noble task. One day, Shab met those women. Shab was surprised to see the number of women as if a sultanate was only for women. This task was difficult but not impossible, it was necessary to have some knowledge. And Shab had done this work very intelligently.

"All of you... don't worry you are free... please give all your information to Abtin and Anosh, who will take you safely to your home."

"You have proved to be an angel to us….Can we know about you?" said a woman.

Shab started thinking that if I give my information, then I will take the trouble for free. Then this trouble will harm everyone which I do not want.

 "After knowing me, what will you do? I think you all should go back to your home and keep yourself safe, careful always!" Shab said.

No one knows what will happen next, but it is good if some lives are saved. When will this end, Shab doesn't know, but a single effort can do something and that was enough for her.

Shab further handed over the work to Abtin and Anosh. Shab was very happy. Today she was proud of herself. For the first time, he was feeling very happy. Shab went to Arsya. Arsya was silent. Shab felt strange. Whenever Arsya looked at Shab, she was always ready to tell many things but why is she silent today? Shab asked Arsya.

 "Khaleh (Aunt) why are you silent? is everything alright?"
"Thank God! We have a special guest here... And it is good to be silent in their service..!"
"Special guest……? But who can be special to you more than me..?" Shab said with a laugh.

 "Look…just after you…." said Arsya.
Shab was shocked to see Baba, Riza, and Shazmaan. How did Shazmaan come to know about here?
"How are you all here? I mean how did you know I'm here…?" Shab's words were falling apart.

"Look…just after you.…" said Arsya.

Shab was shocked to see Baba, Riza, and Shazmaan. How did Shazmaan "Shab… My child… don't get angry like that and now just go to the palace… like this no princess, and Zahedan's queen should leave her people and palace… and I want you not to disobey me. Shazmaan's mother misses you and her condition is not good." Baba tried to convince Shab.

Even before Shab could say anything, Baba banned not saying anything in front of Shab.

"You said right.… Maman, only recite your name with her tongue more than ours. The poor person is on the bed at this age, can neither walk nor get up..!" Riza said, rolling his eyes.

"What happened to Maman…?" asked Shab.

"You'll see for yourself…!" Shazmaan said.

Arsya said to Shab.

"Shab… you must go… Mallika wants to meet you, in such a situation, God's mercy is received … and then his highness himself has come to pick you!"

"And you… can't leave you like that, not at all… If it's a matter of meeting Maman, I and you will meet Maman and come back. I just want to be with you…!"

"Arsya…!" Ammu Baba said.

"Your Highness …?"

"You come with us too…Shab needs you…then you can also do the service of Shazmaan's Maman."

"Yes sir, as you Command."

Shab looked at Shazmaan. Shazmaan was still smiling as if saying that I'm too successful in my motive.
Shab said, "I will go only for Maman…and for Baba!"
Riza could not hold back his laughter. Shazmaan pointed him to keep quiet.

Everyone had reached the palace. The walls of the palace were decorated with roses. There was a celebratory atmosphere everywhere. As Shab entered the palace, Maman was waiting for Shab in a royal dress to welcome Shab. Baba left while saving his eyes and Riza too ... only Shazmaan stood there and Shazmaan bowed his eyes as soon as Shab saw him.

"My sweet child...you don't know how much I missed you!"
"Rightly said, Maman, we were also telling her the same but the princess was not ready to accept it!" Shazmaan said while acting.
"But I didn't say anything… Baba and Riza said that your condition is not good and you were not able to get up from the bed." Shab mentioned.

"Shazmaan, what I'm hearing?" Maman asked.
"Maybe Baba is calling me, I should go, Maman, I'll be right back." Shazmaan left from there.

"Come on, you must be tired, let's take a rest in your room!" Maman said to Shab.
Maman went to her room with Shab. All this was far away from Shab's understanding, after all, what is happening. The room had changed, new clothes, mirrors, and jewelry were present there. The walls were painted white. There were only roses near the window. The room smelled of

rose flowers. Light gold-colored curtains were put on the bed. Shab was surprised to see all this."

"It's your room, Shab! You didn't tell me what happened to you. But I got to know everything. I want you to forget the past and start your new life."
"Maman, I don't want all this and now I have all forgotten, I want to move forward but a simple life is better for me. At least there is peace in it, neither the fear of getting anything nor the fear of losing anything. Pardon me! I want to forget all this along with my old memories.
"Just tell me Maman! Where there is no peace, is there any importance of all these things? I'm happy with Arsya Khaleh; she takes care of me like my Maman." Shab said.

"What about me? Am I not your Maman? I know that you don't want to have any relationship with Shazmaan. But think about whether Shazmaan is really to blame? I believe that you have been completely transformed because of the behavior you have been treated with. Your every wish and hope has come to an end. But look at me too; I never gave up my hope. Today I'm handing over my Shazmaan to you. There is a cure for external wounds and pain, but when something touches the heart, it is very difficult to cure. I have seen Shazmaan suffocating inside… he has been looking for you a lot. He used to go to the garden every day and spend all his time taking care of the flowers. Many times he told me that he was to blame… His wrong decision had caused a lot of trouble for Shab. It is easy to end the relationship but it is difficult to carry it till the last breath. Still, if you feel that I am saying something wrong then we will not stop you from going back and if you stay here then you will appreciate my decision. In the evening, we have a celebration. It is special for you. I hope that you will be there." Maman said to Shab and Maman went to Hall.

 "If I stay here, the purpose I want to fulfill… will remain unfinished. If I mentioned it to anyone, even they would not believe it. What should I do now.....how to inform Abtin and Anosh....where have you trapped me....you didn't do it right Shazmaan! Oh God, what should I do now?

Shab was thinking when Arsya came there.
"Shab I'm going to Vashnam-e-Dari and will come back after doing some work, don't worry about anything!" Arsya said.
"But what is such a necessity? ,
"Shazmaan's Maman ordered me that I should always be with her, there is only some stuff that has to be brought here from there. Servants are also going with me to help."
"Khalch! Give this letter to Abtin and Anosh. It is very important for them." Shab said.
"Baleh!"
"Mamnoon!"

Shab's burden lightened. It was evening time. Shab did not want to disobey Maman, so started preparing for the celebration. Never even a better dress she wore and today because of Maman, she has a priceless dress. Other things like jewelry, henna, and kohl scent. Very deeply the zircon work was done in the dress. The color of the dress is deep Red, just like a rose. Today, in the true sense, she seemed to be the Mallika of Zahedan.

The maid-servants called Shab in the celebration hall where Baba, Riza, Farzin, Maman, and Shazmaan were already present. Such a celebration happened for the first time in the palace in which everyone was happy. There was neither resentment nor coercion. Call it Bazm Arusi or Bazm —e-Aish. It was difficult to say. As soon as Shab came, everyone's eyes were fixed on Shab and everyone had the same word "Wow, So beautiful!". Maman was very happy, seeing Shab and Baba too. Shab put Maman's hand on the forehead with respect and then kissed her hand. You are the most important for me, this is its sign.

Maman said to Shab
"Aha! Well done, my Child!... Look, that naughty is not taking his eyes off you."
"Naughty? Who's that naughty?" Shab asked.
"My son with sky-blue eyes!" and Maman laughed.
"Oh, now I understood... the naughty one is Shazmaan!" Shab said jokingly.

"I'm very happy Shab that you didn't disobey me. Mamnoon!" Maman said and kissed Shab's forehead. "Don't embarrass me Maman......I thank god that I got you who love me more than my family and now I will follow your words. I used to complain to God often that's why God took away the love of my Valedayan from me, today God listened to my complaint and sent me back to you guys. I'm realizing the importance of a family."

"I'm always with you Shab....always....look Shazmaan and Riza cannot tolerate our love and they both are coming here..." Maman said.

"Maman, please join us in your love," said Riza in a mischievous manner.

"Of course, I will but before that, I want that Shazmaan and Shab should spend time together. After all this celebration is special for them Jashn-e-Arusi (Wedding Celebration)."

Saying this, Riza and Maman left them alone. Shazmaan sat down beside Shab... and slowly said to Shab.

"Today I was looking for roses in the garden...but I didn't find them...You know why?" Shazmaan asked Shab.

"Why?"

"Because...the real rose is sitting with me in this gathering.... Shazmaan said.

"Do you think I will be interested in this poetry style of yours? It is a waste of time." Shab said.

"I think you must have eaten something strange in Dirman and Vashnam-e-Dari, because of which your mood always seems to be bad...... maybe you ate the meat of an eight-legged sea animal. Of course an octopus! Exactly, in the same manner, you talk as it repeatedly throws its ink at others." Shazmaan said.

"Hh hhh hhh...it so funny I can't stop laughing...Prince...look my stomach is hurting." Shab said jokingly.

"It's enough Shab! Everyone is seeing this childish act of yours." Shazmaan said.

"Oh! I have forgotten...Today I should be shy. Okay, I bow my eyes...but I will remember your words...and I can't stop laughing." Shab said.

"I know why you are doing this? So, that I walk away from you!" Shazmaan said.

"When were we close prince?"

"Shab...man mikhaham ta aabad ba ta basham (I want to be with you always).

Ba man ezdevaz mikoni (Will you marry me?)......Shab?" Shazmaan asked.

"Do you think all this is a joke?" Shab asked Shazmaan.

"I'm not kidding; I want to make a fresh start. Don't you want me to be with you forever?" Shazmaan said.

"I do not understand anything. At one stage you say that you have nothing to do with me, then how did this change happen so quickly?" Shab asked.

"If you want to know then come with me once...I want to show you something that only you have the right to know and no one else." Shazmaan mentioned.

"Why...I go with you...is there any paradise view?" Shab said

"Come for once, princess... It is my request to you..." Shazmaan said. And both of them left the celebration and went to their room. Shazmaan opened a door and the view outside the door was nothing less than a paradise. The Maah (moon) was spreading its mahtab (moonlight) to the windows of the palace. The place was full of roses. Fireflies were also lighting up everywhere. And those two white birds were present there that had come and sat on Shazmaan's side. That place smelled good. There was only peace there.

Shazmaan told Shab.

"Meet these two birds, my friends….Before I met you they were sitting outside our room's window and when I went to Nikshahar…..they were still with me. When I, Baba, and Riza went out for a walk, I saw you in the garden. I felt that fragrance that day too…I used to forget everything from that fragrance … and this fragrance made me realize that the God I never believed was sending me the signs of my companion. All this disappeared after you left. But when you are here again today, all these have come back. All I want to say is that God has some noble intentions. Or else we can say that both of us are the soul to whom God wants to join." Shazmaan said to Shab.

Shab got lost somewhere in the thought. All this was surprising. If there was any reality in this, then Shab also felt something like this, but Shab did not feel like this. Shab was silent.

"What are you thinking...?"

"Hh…you said something? Umm…khabam miyad (I feel sleepy)! Allow me!" Shab asked Shazmaan.

" It is allowed!"

"Mamnoon!" Shab be kheyr! Shab said.

"Shab be kheyr!" Shazmaan said.

Chapter 14.

"What news have you brought...?"
"Mallika…..Princess Shab is back in the palace...There was a celebration in Qasr-e-kand for princess Shab, there is a celebration for the whole six days. We have special news... Our men are found unconscious and even finding the ship becomes difficult. Not a single eyelet is being found. Neither women nor ships and goods." The informer said.

"There must be a hand of some special person in this. He is a person with too much knowledge. Otherwise, who can show so much courage? He is aware of every corner of this land…. Find out who he is….?" Sultana said.

"But it will take many days to investigate this. Some of our people have also decided that they will go back to their respective countries. If the matter comes out, everyone will be killed." The informer said.
"I think of something else... Till then you and other fellow keep giving me the news of Qasr-e-kand."

"As you command!" said the informer.
There was a fear in Sultana's mind. May this trouble become the reason for her death? This has never happened before. But whoever he is, he is very dangerous for Sultana. His identification is very important. Sultana will

end his life before he becomes the reason for Sultana's death.

98

SHAZMAAN-E-SHAB

end his life before he becomes the reason for Sultana's death.

Chapter 15.

"What news have you brought...?"
"Mallika.….Princess Shab is back in the palace...There was a celebration in Qasr-e-kand for princess Shab, there is a celebration for the whole six days. We have special news... Our men are found unconscious and even finding the ship becomes difficult. Not a single eyelet is being found. Neither women nor ships and goods." The informer said.

"There must be a hand of some special person in this. He is a person with too much knowledge. Otherwise, who can show so much courage? He is aware of every corner of this land…. Find out who he is….?" Sultana said.

 "But it will take many days to investigate this. Some of our people have also decided that they will go back to their respective countries. If the matter comes out, everyone will be killed." The informer said.
"I think of something else... Till then you and other fellow keep giving me the news of Qasr-e-kand."

"As you command!" said the informer.
There was a fear in Sultana's mind. May this trouble become the reason for her death? This has never happened before. But whoever he is, he is very dangerous for Sultana. His identification is very important. Sultana will

end his life before he becomes the reason for Sultana's
death.

Chapter 16.

"If I will be failed, I will destroy them too. I will destroy them like this; neither will be able to cry nor will be able to talk about their devastation to anyone." Sultana said.

"The news is hundred percent true… After the arrival of Shahzadi Shab, Sultan Shazmaan of Zahedan soon announced that the criminals would not get the generosity of life. Many Sultanates have joined them. Some of the sultans even gave death sentences to our men. And the rest fled to their country. The movement of the ships which used to come for the market has been stopped. The army is strictly guarded everywhere. But this is also thankful. That your name hasn't come out yet." The informer said.

"Goth man, do you want my name to come out…..I cannot tolerate all this. Set that palace on fire. No one should be spared. For this work, only choose a person who will not take pity on anyone. When the people of the palace are no more, then nothing will be left for Shazmaan, neither the Sultanate nor the family. No one is more than the ruler of Ardashir. Create havoc in Qasr-e-kand." said the Sultana to her men.

Sultana's spies and her army set out to surround Qasr–e-kand from all sides. It was not difficult for the army to travel far. Ardashir was not aware of this. Destruction will also start on that day when they enter the border of Qasr-e-kand. They were so cunning that no one knew about their arrival, but there would be destruction.

On the other hand, Shazmaan was leaving for Zahedan. Riza asked to accompany but Shazmaan refused, citing Farzin and the palace. Going to Zahedan was also very important. Shazmaan met Shab. Shab was in the garden at that time.

"Sobh be kheyr!"Shazmaan said.
"Sobh be kheyr….Sultan!"
"I'm leaving for Zahedan. It will take five days, yet I will try to come soon. As you are now Mallika, you are now given many responsibilities in the palace."

"But right now! I'm not worthy and even I'm not aware of the ways of a Mallika. I can't handle all this!" Shab said.

"Shab...I know you deserve it...and you can take the education of it from Maman. To become a Mallika, it is enough to be brave. All this is just a small thing for a person who can free slave women."

"Is it really important for you? Without you, the meeting can be arranged."

"If it was not necessary, I would have taken you with me for a trip to Zahedan…and then it is only a matter of five days.….it is getting late, I should leave, and you will take care. Everything now is handed over to you."

"Sultan, Promise me that you will come as soon as possible, without you, I feel empty and alone in this Palace!"

"Of course, I will Shab."
"May God keeps you safe...always...!" Shab said.
"I will tell you one more story after my arrival!" Shazmaan said while caressing Shab's hair.
Shab started smiling at this point.
"I'll be waiting for you...!" Shab said.
"Khuda Hafiz...!"
"Khuda Hafiz..!"

It was difficult to say. But Shab was saddened by Shazmaan's departure. At first, Shab stayed away from Shazmaan. Today Shazmaan is away, so it is as if she has been separated. Five days were equal to five years.

"If this is my condition... then what would be the condition of Shazmaan? Shazmaan stayed away from me for many days. Maman told the truth. Shazmaan used to talk about me. That means I too had troubled him. It means I'm too selfish. Keep thinking about myself." Shab was thinking about all this then Arsya came there. Arsya gave a letter to Shab. The decoration of the letter was made on sight and it smelled of rose perfume.

"This letter for you...!"
"Who sent...?"
"See yourself...!" Arsya said and left from there.
Shab opened the letter and started reading it.

"Hope this letter is being read by the beautiful eyes of Shab...I have written it, especially for you! I also did not want to go to Zahedan,

but for a time there must be a distance between us So that we can understand each other's importance. I used to get scared by the name of Ezdevaaj. You must be wondering how Shazmaan has changed! You are the reason for this. You shook my soul from within. For some time I considered myself guilty. How could be I so heartless?

I didn't want to punish you. But you completed that sentence without revolting. In anger, I did a mistake. I realized later that I should not have done this. I also punished myself mentally. You were sure somewhere that I would make a better decision. I came to know that you value me. Thank you very much for coming into my life! Don't ever distance yourself from me. This is my request to you. Please wait for me!"

Shazmaan-e-Shab

After reading the letter, Shab's eyes got into tears. Two days passed. Then four days. Shab used to go to the garden and read the letter every day. But now the waiting time is about to end. Shab would repeatedly ask Riza about Shazmaan. It hasn't even been five days yet. Anosh's letter comes to Shab the same day.

"Salaam, Mallika of Zahedan!

For the past 2 days, we were continuing the investigation near the Ocean.

We have heard something that there might be a heavy attack on Qasr-e-kand..!

That is why we have sent you this letter as a precaution.

This conspiracy can be done by knowing someone.

*The investigation is still on and we will try our best to reveal the face
of the real culprit soon."*

Khuda Hafiz!

Shab was reading the letter when she heard a serviceman
talking to Riza.

"Some unknown people are crossing the border of Qasr-e-
kand and our army has left in an attempt to stop them.
They are making only the people of Qasr-e-kand their
prey."

"But who are these people… who want to spoil the peace
of the Sultanate… still one more day is left for Dadash to
come and all this is happening in his absence," Riza said.

"Riza…..if they have crossed the border, it will not take
them much time to reach the palace. I want Baba, Maman,
and Farzin to leave the servants of the palace for the south
direction as soon as possible. I will send the rest of the
servants through the secret road of the palace towards
Dirman."

"And you…Nah! I can't do that, can't leave you alone.
What will I answer to Dadash?"

"Riza time is very less…I'm concerned about you all and
you know Farzin's condition, if something happens to
Farzin or Baba, Maman then what will be the answer you
and I will give to Shazmaan. Get the ride ready and take
everyone off here as soon as possible. I can protect myself
and you know this much better than me!" Shab said.

"But still…I don't feel right about this princess!"

"Listen carefully Riza…if I save my life and leave everyone
else here to die, no one is more selfish than me…. This life

is not free... Before that I give you the order as a Mallika, you go with Baba, Maman, and Farzin, Arsya...! Time is less, and as soon as you cross the border of Qasr-e-kand, turn to Zahedan.

Shazmaan will meet you there...and then I will also come there. If I can't return then you and Shazmaan find me with your army... We should hurry." Shab said.
"I will say to Dadash that you are very stubborn..." said Riza with a laugh.
"Khuda Hafiz! Be safe always Riza!" Shab said.
Shab started sending everyone from the palace to the secret place. Shab gave Riza her book on his way and a letter...which was the same as Shazmaan had sent for Shab. Shab said while giving the map to Riza.

"These maps will help you.....and give this letter to Shazmaan. If I'm successful here then I will come there or else I will wait for Shazmaan."
"We will keep praying for your well-being...." Said Riza and left from there. Shab had almost taken everyone to the secret road. There was noise in the city; the sound of shouting was coming everywhere. For a moment, Shab was stunned and began to lead everyone towards the path leading to the garden, when a loud explosion damaged the upper part of the palace. Riza on his way saw the palace. There was fire everywhere. Those who were setting the palace on fire only realized that the people of the palace had been converted into ashes here. Every corner of the palace was set on fire. Nothing remains.... This devastation was in front of Shab's eyes. But the comfort was that the people of the palace were safe.

The towers of the palace were burning. There was looting among the people. It seemed that some storm came and ruined everything. Shab started looking for a safe place along with the servicemen and palace people. It was a short distance away that a dagger had passed through Shab's body. When she looked back, she saw the big eyes of Sultana in a dark dress. Sultana started laughing.
"I was looking for you!" Sultana said.

And gestured to her residents and asked them to go back. Saying this, she ran away from there.
Some amount of blood had come out of Shab's body. Her eyes were turning red. The wound was deep. It is also difficult to get up and walk. A Khidmatgar (servant) placed the Shab on a plank and tied the wound with a piece of cloth.

"All of you should go out from here…it is useless to worry about me….,
Shab said to the Khidmatgar (servants).

"You have saved all of us without caring about your life. We cannot leave you."
"In my entire life, I kept praying for my death… But today when I want to live, then God does not approve of it."
Shab was tolerating the pain. Time was short. But she still hoped that Shazmaan would come. But the hope did not succeed for long. She looked at the night with open eyes which were silent without a moon.
Shab's body had completely cooled.

Shazmaan had reached Qasr-e-kand. Riza was found on the way. Riza sent Maman and Farzin, Baba to Nikshahar instead of Zahedan. Seeing the condition of Qasr-e- kand,

Shazmaan asked Riza.

"How did all this happen and who did it...?"

"Don't know dadash!"

"Maman, Baba, Farzin and Shab are safe?"

"Maman, Baba and Farzin are in Nikshahar,

"And Shab...?" When Shazmaan asked, Riza bowed his head.

"Riza you left Shab alone….how can you do all this? ,

"I explained a lot to her but she needed to save everyone's life". Riza said.

When a servant saw Shazmaan and Riza, he took them to Shab in Kamingah. Shazmaan did not delay.
Shazmaan said to Shab.

"Shab... I have come as promised. Let's get up now. ,
Had she been there, she would have got up. Shab's dress was stained with blood. But Shazmaan still could not believe it. Riza could not see his condition. Shazmaan took Shab's hand in his hand which was like Ice.
"I told you to wait for me… but you are still silent."
Riza said while handling Shazmaan
"Dadash……Shab is no more…" Riza said.

This time was not less than any trouble for Shazmaan. It was difficult for him to forget Shab. Many days passed, and a year passed.

"Finally your words were completed….You said that one day you will go so far away from me that only your name will remain and you have shown it by doing it. Shab I remained where I was…!" Shazmaan often started talking to himself.

This time has passed. The result of this conspiracy of Sultana was the death sentence. Shazmaan is no longer the same. He left the Sultanate. He found it appropriate to offer prayers. Zahedan was handed over to Riza. Maman could not bear the shock. Ammu Baba's condition is no longer the same, been sick often. Farzin was busy with her child.

But without Shab, Shazmaan was again incomplete. In the name of Shab, Shazmaan made a huge garden of roses and started living there, and talking to roses. That was his life now. One day Riza came to Shazmaan.

"Dadash, I want to give something to you….seeing your condition, I didn't give it to you at that time. But today I like it better….if you didn't give it then maybe my soul will not forgive me!… This book in which the princess Shab left a letter for you." Said Riza
Shazmaan opened the book which contained his letter and started reading Shab's letter.

I was wondering that

A great man will fall in my love

I thought u have heart of stone

But I found you very soft-hearted.

Yes, I want to be your...but not only in this life, but also afterlife forever.

I accept your proposal to always be together.

Now I believed that God makes us only for each other.

This is not only love...This is pure love.

And I'm your night ...I can't adore myself without you. You are the only one who makes me special...that's why everyone says:

Shazmaan-E-Shab

SHAB-E-SHAZMAAN

"You promised me that you would wait for me ..."
Shazmaan said slowly and from the sky two white birds sat beside Shazmaan and bring that fragrance back! This gives the feeling of Shab's existence even though Shab is not there!

****